SEE HER DIE

Copyright © 2013 Debra Webb, Pink House Press
2003 "Protective Instincts," Harlequin

ISBN: 1508751714
ISBN 13: 9781508751717

PINK HOUSE PRESS
WebbWorks
Huntsville, Alabama

SEE HER DIE

DEBRA WEBB

PINK
HOUSE
PRESS

This book is dedicated to my husband, Nonie Webb, who has trusted me from day one and has allowed me to follow my dream. Forever would never be long enough to spend with you.

PROLOGUE

"Now who's in control, Ned?"

The razor sharp edge of the dagger she held glistened in the light. Ned tried to speak…to beg, to tell her he would do anything she asked, but he couldn't. He could only mumble through the scrunched-up panties she'd forced into his mouth.

Why had he allowed her into his apartment? He should have realized something was wrong but she'd distracted him.

He'd made a terrible, terrible mistake.

"Oh, that's right," she said, her voice condescending, as she trailed the metallic tip down the center of his chest. A creeping, crawling shiver followed its path. "You can't talk right now, can you?"

She smiled a sick, sinister smile—one he wouldn't have associated with her. He tried to swallow, gagging on the silk choking him. His eyes burned. He was a grown, man and he was going to cry.

Why the hell was she doing this?

Sweat coated his skin. His heart pounded harder, making his chest ache, as she walked all the way around him. Please, please, he prayed, let this be just another of her games. He didn't want to die like this, naked and tied to a chair.

He didn't want to die at all.

"If they found you like this," she continued, her tone casual, as if tying up a man at gunpoint and then waving a dagger in his face was an everyday affair, "maybe they'd recognize you for the pervert you are." She checked the rope binding his wrists behind his back. He tried to pull away.

Ned closed his eyes and fought another sting of tears. Surely she couldn't mean to—

"Look at me, *Dr.* Harrison."

He opened his eyes. She stood in front of him now, the tip of the blade pressed against the flesh directly over his heart. It thundered savagely. So hard he could scarcely draw a breath.

What had he done to her that was so bad? She'd enjoyed the sex just as much as he had. He'd ended the brief affair, as he always did, on an upbeat note and she hadn't complained. Why now?

"All those women, Ned." She shook her head in disapproval. "You're a user," she snarled. "You strike when your prey is the most vulnerable. You're nothing but scum."

He whimpered, the sound small and desperate. No! He refused to play the victim for her. He wanted to scream. To remind her that she had come to him!

They'd all been willing. He hadn't forced any of them. They'd liked it...wanted it!

The tip of the blade pierced his flesh. He felt the warm blood bloom, then ooze down his chest. Felt the tears spill from his eyes. Something like a sob escaped his aching throat. This couldn't be happening to him. Not now.

She laughed, the sound brittle and harsh. "You bastard, you're not a man. You're a coward. A real man wouldn't have to prey on vulnerable women. A *real man* wouldn't cry when faced with the truth." She poked him a little harder, drawing blood again.

A muffled cry emerged before he could stop it.

"You're sick. That's what you are. What's next for the great doctor? Little girls waiting at the bus stop?"

He stilled. The realization hit him like a bus barreling down Sixth Avenue. So that was what this was all about. She was pissed off because—dear God, could it be that simple? He snorted, then laughed as best he could with those frigging panties shoved halfway down his throat. What a stupid bitch. What the hell had she expected?

Fury darkened her face. "Are you laughing at me?"

He tried to control himself, but he just couldn't stop. If he hadn't been tied to the chair, he would have doubled over with the laughter bubbling up inside him.

"You son of a bitch."

He laughed, and then coughed, almost choking. All *this* was about one stupid little slut.

"Go to hell!" She lunged, jamming the dagger into his chest.

His body jerked as his startled gaze collided with hers.

She looked as surprised as he was.

Shaking her head, she backed away from him.

He blinked, then stared down at his chest. The jewel-handled weapon was buried to the hilt.

Damn.

He looked up at her one last time as the narrow focus of death closed in around him.

She'd killed him.

CHAPTER ONE

Elizabeth Young imagined that Dr. Ned Harrison was every bit as good-looking in death as he'd been in life. The white linen that draped his coffin, along with the six tall candles surrounding it, made an impressive display. But the most effective ploy was the huge choir assembled behind the distinguished looking priest. The choir's grand entrance, as well as the blessing, had been nothing short of awe-inspiring. And Elizabeth wasn't even Catholic.

The brooding medieval architecture of the Holy Trinity Church lent a dramatic atmosphere for his final public appearance. It was the perfect sendoff for such a highly regarded, nationally renowned psychiatrist.

No one who knew him, least of all Elizabeth, would be at all surprised to find Ned's picture on the social page of tomorrow's issue of the *New York Times*. The city would mourn the loss of a brilliant

1

doctor, and a great number of its female inhabitants would mourn him for completely different reasons.

Elizabeth surveyed the crowd around her as the priest continued to celebrate Mass in solemn, hushed tones. More than half of those present were women under forty, fashionably dressed, all beautiful and probably all wealthy.

Though she was neither rich nor glamorous, she would bet her next month's earnings the one thing all the females gathered had in common was that they had slept with the deceased.

Including Elizabeth.

Knowing full well there was no getting comfortable physically or mentally, she shifted on the hard wooden pew. What on earth had possessed her to come to Ned's funeral Mass? She glanced around at the other women, all facing forward in somber attention, and wondered what *their* reasons for making an appearance might be. Maybe, rather than mourning or showing their respect, they'd all come for the same very personal reason—to make absolutely certain the bastard was dead.

Of course, the visit the homicide detectives had paid Elizabeth had pretty much driven the point home. The two men had been fairly cordial at first, but the questions had soon turned openly accusing, as had their attitudes. She hoped she wouldn't have to go through that again. She had a new life here, a clean, fresh start.

She'd almost allowed Ned Harrison to ruin everything. Her heart squeezed painfully.

How could she have been so foolish?

"Can you believe she wore that dress to a funeral?"

Elizabeth snapped from her pity party and turned to the woman sitting next to her, her one trusted friend. "What?" she whispered.

Gloria Weston angled her head to the right in a gesture that made Elizabeth want to hunker down out of sight. "Over there. The blond in the fiery red dress," Gloria muttered under her breath.

Elizabeth strained to look without actually moving her head. She frowned. "Do you know her?" The woman looked vaguely familiar, but Elizabeth couldn't quite place her.

Gloria shook her head. "She looks like that model who got into trouble last year. I don't know. She's probably just another one of Ned's hussies."

Elizabeth cocked an eyebrow. "What does that make us?"

Gloria snorted softly. Fortunately no one seemed to notice the rude sound. "Fools," she retorted. "Just like the rest of them."

Elizabeth didn't want to think about that—or the phone call she'd gotten from Ned that Friday afternoon. The slime ball. He'd called two or three times that week, begging her to have dinner with him. *Just to talk*, he'd assured her. *I'm not ready to let you go*, he'd added in that charismatic voice of his. What a jerk. She knew what he wanted all right, and she had no intention of falling into that trap again.

No way.

But then, she'd gone to the restaurant anyway. He'd made her an offer she couldn't refuse. Her pulse quickened at the thought of the video. It was the only reason she'd gone, and then he hadn't shown up. She'd wanted to kill him. Elizabeth felt sick to her stomach at the memory. Who'd have thought that less than two weeks later she'd be attending his funeral? It was eerie.

What if the detectives had found…?

No. She resisted the urge to shake her head. She refused to go there.

"Look." Gloria nodded toward another woman who sat two rows up. This one had coal black hair cut in one of those sleek, face-hugging styles. She sported a dress that defied any description Elizabeth might have attempted.

"That's Vanessa Bumbalough," Gloria said, one hand over her mouth.

The name didn't ring a bell. The woman sat next to a man who resembled Johnny Depp in profile. He hadn't bothered to remove his sunglasses. Elizabeth's brow furrowed in question as she leaned closer to her friend. "Who's Vanessa whatever-you-said?"

The man sitting directly behind them cleared his throat. Elizabeth cringed. Gloria ignored him. "She's a new big deal fashion designer. She's all over the papers lately. Don't you ever read?" Gloria made an impatient face. "Apparently her designs stole the show at this season's big fashion debut. The whole industry's up in arms. She's hot hot hot."

4

Ned wouldn't have chosen her otherwise, Elizabeth mused. The man had a reputation to maintain, after all. She winced at the idea of just how gullible she had been. How could she have thought that Ned Harrison was really interested in her? She wasn't beautiful in the classic sense of the word, though she wasn't exactly unattractive. Her social graces left a lot to be desired. She couldn't tolerate contact lenses, leaving her no alternative but to wear glasses. Even worse, she'd done the unthinkable by giving up a prestigious job at a ritzy interior design firm and taken blue-collar work. Not a good thing in a city where profession was the single most qualifying factor for being a part of the *in* crowd.

Screw the in crowd. Elizabeth was happy just as she was—for the most part.

She glanced at her friend. Gloria was one of the city's beautiful people. Petite, a head of feisty red corkscrew curls, pixie features. A power job on Wall Street. People loved her. She was the first friend Elizabeth made when she arrived in the city. She'd met her at one of Brian's, her ex-fiancé's, infamous parties. Gloria had been there for Elizabeth since. Through the breakup with Brian, leaving the firm, and having to find a new, low rent place to live, in addition to finding work.

Ned the-Casanova-shrink Harrison had almost cost Elizabeth that friendship and he definitely was not worth it.

Then again, he hadn't deserved to be murdered either. A trickle of guilt followed on the heels of that thought. She couldn't deny experiencing just a little glee when she'd read about his abrupt demise in last Sunday's paper, but then she was only human. The idea that she'd spoken with him only hours before his unfortunate date with destiny was completely unnerving. What if he'd actually shown up for their dinner date and laid on the charm? What if she'd fallen under his spell one last time?

Last being the operative word. Her mind conjured up the murder scene the newspaper had described in grim detail and her stomach roiled.

Dying in such a humiliating manner was overkill, no pun intended. Sure, there'd been a moment or two when she could have killed him herself, but the truth was she was an adult. It wasn't like Dr. Harrison had taken advantage of a helpless child. She'd made a conscious decision to enter into a sexual relationship with him. As had, she presumed, most of those assembled here today. She scanned the seated crowd of women who could easily fill several issues of *Vogue* or *Cosmo.*

As the priest began the eulogy, his opening remarks bemoaned the great man New York City had lost. Elizabeth wondered if the kindly Father would have waxed so eloquently if he'd had a loved one who'd been one of Ned's conquests.

"Look." Gloria inclined her head toward the aisle that separated the rows of pews. "Remember her from the party the other night?"

Elizabeth peeked past her friend to the woman in question as she scooted in at the end of a row. The rustle of silk and lightweight wool accompanied the efforts of those already seated to accommodate the late arrival. The woman was tall, impossibly thin and, of course, beautiful. Elizabeth did remember her. She was an actress. She'd just landed some big part in a movie. Elizabeth nodded in response to her friend's expectant expression.

She remembered the party, too. She hated those kinds of parties, but Gloria dragged her to them all the same. Hardly a weekend passed without some sort of party Gloria insisted they simply could not miss. Luckily they'd only run into Brian once or twice. Wherever they went the crowd was always the same: a little too wild for Elizabeth's liking. Gloria called her a party pooper. The truth was, Elizabeth was simply a homebody. She wasn't into the party scene the way Gloria and her other friends were.

Besides, it had been only ten months since she and Brian parted ways. That was entirely too long in Gloria's opinion for Elizabeth to still be afraid to go out on a limb with someone new. Elizabeth didn't see it that way. In spite of her mother's desertion, she had been raised in a small town where people mated for life, not for one night. Elizabeth would be the first to admit that Brian had not been the love of her life. He'd been a means to an end. She just hadn't recognized that reality until it was too late.

Moving to New York had been the right thing to do. Breaking out on her own was also the right thing to do, even if it had been scarier than hell at first. She had survived.

She'd survived Ned Harrison, too, hadn't she? How could Gloria have expected her to look for a new love when Elizabeth had gotten so tangled up in Ned's web of deceit? She shook off the disturbing thoughts. She was a survivor. That was what her daddy always said, and her daddy had been a very smart man.

Moistening her lips to conceal the tiny smile thoughts of her father evoked, Elizabeth straightened and focused her attention on the priest's words. She was here. She might as well pay attention. She darted a look at her friend. Gloria appeared to have finally settled in now that she'd scrutinized the crowd. A mixture of affection and respect bloomed in Elizabeth's chest. Gloria was in a league of her own. It seemed impossible that Ned, the heartless bastard, had fooled her. Maybe even Gloria had her vulnerable spot.

Ned Harrison had been an expert at finding those spots.

Elizabeth drew in a heavy breath. They'd both survived Ned—but would *she* survive his murder? What if the police discovered her secret?

Special Agent Collin MacBride paid little attention to the priest's words as he continued his evaluation of the attendees. The group was a veritable who's who from the city's high society and the up-and-coming. Mostly women. No surprise there.

Mac watched one woman in particular. Elizabeth Young. He shifted slightly so that he could see her better. Tall, slender. She wore a black dress, though not the kind one expected to see at a funeral. Then again, none of the women present were dressed in proper mourning attire. Things had definitely changed since his days as an altar boy. He'd seen enough long, shapely legs and silk fabric to feel as if he'd stepped into the middle of a competition for the next top model, rather than a nave filled for a funeral service. Amid the variations of in vogue sameness was Elizabeth Young.

She was decidedly different.

Tall, even wearing flat-heeled shoes, she didn't walk with the same confident glide as the others. No nail polish, very little makeup. He'd gotten a pretty good look at her when she first entered the church. He'd been standing in the shadows near the massive double doors. She and her friend, one Gloria Weston, had hurried to find a seat as if they feared they might miss the opening act of the hottest new Broadway play.

Elizabeth Young wore glasses, the small, gold-wire-rimmed kind. Oddly enough, there was something appealing about the prim look the eyewear gave her, or maybe it was the braid restraining her long hair. He cocked an eyebrow at the direction his meandering thoughts had taken. He'd definitely gone too many hours without sleep. Anytime he looked at a possible suspect and found her appealing in some way, he needed to recharge his batteries. Years of training and field experience weren't supposed to just fly out the window. Where was his focus? Down the toilet, obviously, along with his patience for bumbling homicide detectives. He gritted his teeth when he considered how badly they'd screwed up on this one.

Next to him, Luke Duncan edged a bit closer and spoke in a low voice, "She doesn't really look like the type who could bury a knife in a man's chest."

Mac glanced at his brand-new partner, a kid on his first field assignment. Luke had a lot to learn that only experience on the ground would teach him. "They usually don't," Mac assured him.

What the hell did he think? That a killer walked around with an identifying mark stamped on his or her forehead?

Duncan shrugged, too cocky to be embarrassed. "I mean, she just doesn't look like the type who screws around with some guy, then sticks him."

Still waters ran deep more often than not, Mac considered, but said, "Harrison's murder was an emotional kill, an act of passion. You saw the video. Miss Young is certainly capable of the necessary emotion."

"Man, is she," Duncan muttered wistfully.

Mac clenched his jaw as the images he'd watched on that video quickly played in the private theater of his mind. Oh yeah, Elizabeth Young was definitely passionate. His pulse quickened as his mind focused on one particularly vivid image of her nude body. Streaks of gold highlighted her lush brown mane as it glided over her skin with her rhythmic movements atop her lover. Small, firm breasts jutting forward, begging to be tasted. She might not have that high-class walk down pat, but she damn sure had the art of sex down to a science. His body reacted to the memory.

He looked away, silently cursing himself. Elizabeth Young wasn't just a suspect, she was the prime suspect in this high-profile murder investigation. He didn't need a case of lust where she was concerned. The facts were all he needed. And he had several of those.

Ned Harrison had scheduled a dinner appointment with Elizabeth Young at seven that Friday night. By nine he was dead. The homicide detectives had found the very private, definitely X-rated video of Harrison and Young in his bedroom. Other videos had been found as well, more than two dozen. Ned had been a busy man. Half or so of the videos featured extended sex sessions with former patients. The others involved current patients. All the videos except Elizabeth's had been safely tucked away in his walk-in closet, right behind his wall of Armani and Prada suits. Each had been labeled with a name and date—all except Elizabeth's.

Mac didn't know yet what made hers different but he would find out. *That* she could count on. It was an absolute miracle the NYPD detectives hadn't given away that ace in the hole. At least they'd had sense enough to keep the videos to themselves when conducting their hasty interviews and spilling their guts to the media.

As if that fiasco wasn't enough, the so-called rush on the forensics report that should have been ready yesterday was stuck in a political bottleneck. He'd had to fight like hell to get NYPD to cooperate in this case. It was Wednesday—the vic had been dead twelve days—and Mac hadn't been allowed to interview any witnesses or suspects. Hell, he hadn't even gotten the detectives' reports until this morning. He hated delays. He hated screw-ups even more. One brash detective had royally screwed up by pushing Miss Young until she went on the defensive—the absolute wrong thing to do. What did they teach these guys in detective school?

Mac folded his arms over his chest and seethed.

Now, almost two weeks after the man's murder, he'd finally gotten the go ahead to proceed with his investigation in the case. Local cops didn't like the feds horning in on their territory, but there was no help for it on this one.

Yep, he hated delays, hated not knowing all the available facts. Simple things, like whether Harrison had sex before he died or if he'd been drinking or hitting his drug of choice. The only two things he did know at this point were the approximate time of death and the apparent cause of death. Brannigan, the shoot-first-ask-questions-later detective from the NYPD's Homicide Division, was running down the history of the dagger. Was it a part of Harrison's personal collection? Or had the killer brought it with her or him? Harrison owned an extensive collection of antique swords and daggers, one of which may have been used to send him to hell.

Some hobby. Mac imagined the weapons gave the guy a sense of power. He wondered how powerful he'd felt when one had been jammed deep between his ribs?

Mac hadn't liked Ned Harrison. He liked him even less now that he was dead. It blew Mac's ongoing investigation all to hell. As a member of a special task force he'd been watching Harrison for months, hoping for a break in the illegal and deviant Internet activities of a group known as the Gentlemen's Association. Harrison was the first of the group they'd been able to pinpoint and identify. Now he was dead, leaving Mac back at square one. The Bureau was less than happy with the setback, adding to the frustration of the past twelve days.

It was certainly possible Harrison's death was a well planned and executed hit designed to look like a crime of passion. The head of the Gentlemen's Association may have learned that Harrison had been compromised. Mac couldn't see how anyone could know the feds were onto Harrison. Mac had been too careful. It made more sense that it was just what it appeared to be. Still, before he scrapped Harrison as a primary lead, Mac intended to ensure there was nothing more to be gleaned about the secretive Gentlemen's Association from Harrison's life or his death.

Harrison had risen above his humble foster child beginnings. Both he and his only sibling, a twin brother, had done well for themselves. His brother's death four years ago had left Harrison alone in the world since he'd opted not to marry and have a family of his own. Not surprising in Mac's opinion. Men like Harrison were too selfish for family.

"Our lady is on the move," Duncan warned.

Mac hauled his attention back to the present, his gaze seeking Elizabeth Young. She was working her way to the end of the row, muttering *excuse-me's* to those seated between her and the aisle.

Just where the hell was she going? Heads turned as she dashed down the aisle, past Mac and into the vestibule.

He glanced at Duncan, giving him an unspoken command to stay put. Mac slipped quietly into the large entry hall. Young pushed up her glasses and swiped her eyes, and then wrapped her arms around her middle but not before he saw the tremor in her hands. Had her heinous deed finally pinged her conscience? Or maybe she was just now comprehending all the cops had openly accused her of.

Without making a sound, he stepped closer and offered her the handkerchief from his coat pocket. He never could tolerate a weeping female. "Are you all right?"

Elizabeth stared at the white handkerchief for several seconds before she reluctantly accepted it. "Thank you," she murmured without looking at him. "I'm okay."

Another step disappeared between them. "Did you know him well?"

Her head shot up. She looked straight into his eyes and blinked. "What?"

"Dr. Harrison," he offered, coming closer still. Close enough to watch the pupils of her eyes widen when she realized she was alone with a stranger who was suddenly in her personal space. "I mean," he explained carefully, keeping his voice low, gentle, "you're so upset. I thought perhaps you were family or maybe his girlfriend."

Her fingers clenched the white cotton. She didn't even breathe—at least, not that Mac could see. She looked like a deer caught in the headlights of an oncoming car, frightened and too shocked to react. Her scent filled his senses. Not perfume. Soap or shampoo, he decided. Something soft and sweet and intensely appealing.

She shook her head finally. "No. I'm...a former patient."

Mac shrugged. "I suppose losing your therapist can be overwhelming."

Her gaze narrowed at the hint of sarcasm in his voice. Damn. He hadn't meant to let it slip out.

She looked him up and down for the first time. "I'm sorry, I didn't get your name."

He smiled, the one the ladies always told him they liked. All confidence and charm. If Miss Young liked it, she showed no outward indication. "Collin MacBride." He offered his hand. She ignored it.

Clearly suspicious, she pushed her glasses higher on her nose. "Were *you* one of his patients, too?"

Smart lady. She watched closely for signs of deception. Elizabeth Young might look like the naive librarian who needed to get laid, but she hadn't fallen off the turnip truck just yesterday.

"No," he confessed. "Just a friend."

She shoved the handkerchief back at him without having used it. "Thank you, Mr. MacBride, but I should get back."

"Wait." He stopped her before she could escape. She hesitated at the entryway to the nave and turned back to him. He cranked up the wattage of his smile. "You didn't tell me your name."

Something flickered in those amber eyes, fear, anger, both maybe. "No," she said, her voice tight. "I didn't."

She left him staring after her. However smart she thought she was, whatever cover-up skills she'd learned since the last time she'd stabbed a man in the chest, it wouldn't be enough.

Mac would not give up until he knew everything she'd seen, said, and done where Ned Harrison was concerned.

His smile widened. She had until tomorrow morning.

Then, she was his.

CHAPTER TWO

Mac had given her two days. More than enough time for the shock to fade and the reality of Harrison's death to steep into her conscience. Assuming Elizabeth Young had a conscience. Considering the bout of tears she'd suffered at the funeral, Mac was relatively certain she still had one. Duncan had been right in that respect. Mac really didn't see her as a coldblooded killer. Jealousy could drive people to do things they normally wouldn't. Or maybe she'd found out what Harrison was doing with his videoed sessions. The discovery would piss anybody off.

It was eight a.m. and Mac had opted to leave Duncan yanking Detective Brannigan's chain regarding the origin of the murder weapon. Truth was, Mac preferred questioning a suspect alone the first go-around.

He'd arrived at Elizabeth Young's small Leonia apartment at seven sharp. On the Jersey side of the Hudson, the apartment was actually the attic-turned-living-space portion of an older home owned by an elderly woman who lived alone. According to the landlady, who acted as a sort of answering service, Miss Young had already left for the job site this morning. Another step in the wrong direction for Mac. The most effective interviews were conducted on the suspect's home turf where they were the most comfortable.

Who'd have thought she'd be up and at 'em so damned early?

Mac checked the street and number he'd jotted down. Almost there. He drove past some of the city's finest cast-iron architecture with its ornate facades and over sized windows until he reached the SoHo address the landlady had given him. He parked in a nearby alley and walked to the entrance of the four-story building. Scaffolding and indications of ongoing plaster repair cluttered the would-be lobby. An ancient warehouse turned residential lofts, eight in number, no doubt with price tags to match the upscale address.

He boarded the old-style freight elevator and set it into motion. Despite being in a state of refurbishment, the building, and location were a far cry from Elizabeth Young's current home address. He'd read her poignant Cinderella story. Her defense attorney would use that saga to sway sympathy from the jury when the time came. Small-town girl falls in love with big-city boy and follows her heart in hopes of making her dreams come true. Then, as dreams have a way of doing, they'd crashed down around her. The love of her life had turned out to be a lying, cheating, smooth-talking womanizer.

Poor Elizabeth had suddenly found herself on her own in the big, bad city.

The elevator came to a stop, groaning loudly in protest. Somehow, Mac thought with a twinge of respect that annoyed the hell out of him, she'd managed to land on her feet. She'd found an affordable, yet tolerable place with reasonable rent, and she'd fallen back on the trade she'd learned from her father—painting. Not the artsy kind, but the plain old, elbow-grease-required, refurbishing sort.

In the past eight months she'd built a solid reputation and enough business to merit hiring a helper. Mac walked down the corridor toward the open door on the right. There were two large lofts on each floor, one on either side of the centrally located elevator and corridor. Since the other door was closed, it made sense to go for the open one first.

Her helper would be around here somewhere. She'd picked herself a real winner there, too. Mac wondered if she had any idea the con artist she'd hired had a rap sheet as long as his arm. Then again, her own rap sheet was nothing to scoff at—which was something else they had to discuss. According to Detective Brannigan, the lady didn't like to talk about her past. Mac felt fairly certain she wouldn't care for any of his questions, especially after the report he'd read this morning.

The preliminary report from the medical examiner confirmed that Harrison had sex prior to his death. The only substantial clue as to the identity of the person with whom he'd had sex was a single pubic hair that didn't belong to the deceased. Well, that and a few healthy scratches on his neck that were only a couple of hours old at the time of death. DNA testing was already under way. All they needed was a comparison sample to try for a match.

Miss Young wasn't going to like that part either.

Mac paused in the open doorway and surveyed the scene before him. Keith Beaumont, better known as Boomer to his friends, stood on a ladder using long brush strokes of white paint as he edged the wall around the expansive windows. According to his file, he was just over six feet tall and a wiry hundred and forty pounds. His twenty-second birthday had come and gone a month ago, but his crime-ridden teenage years had left their mark on his thin face. A white scar, which stood out despite his fair complexion, stretched downward from his hairline through his right eyebrow, leaving a permanent part. He'd buzzed his blond hair to the point of baldness. A number of nasty-looking tattoos adorned any visible flesh below his neck. The tattered jeans and black t-shirt completed the untrustworthy picture.

Mac couldn't imagine what Elizabeth saw in the kid, unless it was a kindred spirit. There was no time like the present to ask. His gaze slid across the empty room to her location facing the wall farthest from him. She rolled on the paint in a zigzag pattern, carefully covering the newly re-plastered surface with a fresh coat of pristine white paint. Her hair was secured high on the back of her head in a long ponytail. She wore baggy overalls and a plain white t-shirt. A red shop cloth, stained with a bit of white paint, hung from her right rear pocket.

The image looked incredibly innocent. Another image, one from the video, abruptly appeared before his eyes. He blinked, shattering the picture that had burned into his brain, but not before it had its usual effect. Even with her head thrown back in ecstasy, she looked somehow vulnerable, innocent and every damned muscle in his body reacted.

A muscle pulsed in his jaw. Looks could be deceiving. He was halfway across the room before she sensed someone's presence and turned around.

"Miss Young, I hope this isn't a bad time."

Her surprise immediately turned to annoyance. There was a tiny splatter of paint on the lower edge of one lens of her glasses. Boomer turned to check out their visitor. To his credit he kept his mouth shut. Mac hoped he stayed smart that way.

Elizabeth braced for trouble. She remembered this guy from the funeral. What was his name? Something MacBride. Tall, good-looking, charming. He'd offered her his handkerchief. She remembered he'd smelled as good as he looked. The earthy scent had been subtle but impossible to ignore. What was he doing here? And why was her heart suddenly pounding so hard?

New York City was full of handsome guys. This was the first time one had tracked her down. She squared her shoulders and ignored her silly reaction. Nerves, that was all it could be. She'd had a hell of a week. Maybe the guy needed a painter. If so, he'd come to the right place.

"We met at the funeral," he offered, apparently taking her silence as a sign that she didn't recognize him. "Collin MacBride."

He extended one broad hand and gifted her with the charming smile that was a perfect complement to his polished appearance. The navy suit was obviously tailored just for him, the white shirt crisply starched, and the tie was a rich blue that brought out the color of his eyes. His black leather shoes suggested Italian craftsmanship. Those high dollar soft soles explained how he'd sneaked up on her.

Get it together, Elizabeth. She passed the paint roller and handle to her left hand and swiped her right on the leg of her overalls before accepting his. He was probably just an insurance salesman. Didn't those guys always hang out at funerals?

The zing of electricity that passed between them as their palms touched startled her all over again. She snatched her hand back and instantly went on the defensive. "Do you make a habit of looking up all the women you hit on at funerals, Mr. MacBride?"

One side of that full mouth hitched up a little higher. "Only on occasion, Miss Young."

She resisted the urge to rub her still-sizzling palm against her leg. He was looking at her—no, not just looking—studying her. Who was this guy? When she could bear the scrutiny of those piercing blue eyes no longer, she spoke up, "So what's the occasion?"

He reached into his interior coat pocket and pulled out a black leather case. Her frown deepened with growing confusion, and then she knew. *He was a cop.* Damn. Why hadn't she thought of that? Just what she needed, more questions she couldn't answer about an event she seriously wanted to forget.

He displayed his credentials for her inspection before tucking them back into his pocket. "*Agent* MacBride," he clarified for her benefit in case she hadn't read the fine print on his Federal Bureau of Investigation ID. "I'm looking into the murder of Dr. Ned Harrison. Your landlady said you'd be here."

A draining sensation made her sway before she could recapture her balance. "I've already answered the police's questions. I don't know anything else." Dammit, why did her voice have to sound so shaky?

The paint roller felt suddenly too heavy to hold. She swiveled stiffly and placed it in the pan. Her thoughts raced like a competitor at the Daytona 500 as she straightened. She would need to talk to Mrs. Polk about giving out her whereabouts to strangers. She doubted that would have stopped this man. One flash of his official ID and Mrs. Polk had no recourse but to answer whatever he asked. What did he want with Elizabeth? She'd told the police everything she knew. There was nothing else that needed telling. Not if she could help it.

"I need to clear up a few discrepancies. Routine procedure."

Déja vu hit like a blow to her midsection. The blood on her hands, her ex-brother-in-law screaming in agony. The police handcuffing her and forcing her into the patrol car. Routine procedure often included unjust incarceration. She couldn't afford to miss any more work. The developer would refuse to pay her the remainder of her contract if she failed to finish on time. She had to have these two lofts completed by the end of next week.

She moistened her lips and adopted an outer calm she in no way felt. "I don't know how I can help you, Agent MacBride, but I'll do what I can."

Boomer was watching, his mounting uneasiness radiating clear across the room. She wanted to say something to reassure him, but at the moment she could only stare into the eyes focused so intently on her. Those haunting memories from the past she'd worked so hard to put behind her kept clawing at her shaky determination.

"According to Harrison's appointment book, you were scheduled to have dinner with him at seven the evening he was murdered."

It wasn't a question. He already knew the answer. So did the detectives who'd interrogated her on two different occasions, and still he wanted to analyze her as she answered. This was a man who checked his facts carefully, and made his own measured evaluations. He would never take anyone else's word for anything. He wasn't like the two detectives who'd interviewed her already.

Judging by the set of his broad shoulders and the intensity of his gaze, he already knew more about her than she wanted him to know. Far more than the other detectives had bothered to gather. He'd read her file, made calls, had her pegged as a suspect. He had likely known exactly who she was when he approached her in the church. Dammit she didn't need this right now. She didn't want to go through this kind of emotion-twisting investigation again.

Once in a lifetime was more than enough.

Why had she lost control during the service? She would never convince anyone that it had nothing to do with Ned's death and everything to do with fear for the life she'd worked so hard to build here. Selfish, she knew, but true. It must have looked as if she'd been overcome by grief—or guilt. *The video.* What if he'd found the video? The other two men hadn't mentioned it. Maybe Ned had thrown it away or locked it up somewhere.

"Miss Young?"

"That's right." The words were hers but the voice sounded as if it came from someone else. "But Ned—Dr. Harrison—never showed up at the restaurant."

MacBride slipped his hands into his trouser pockets and inclined his head, his relentless gaze never deviating from hers. "The maître d' confirmed

Harrison never arrived. Where did you go when you left around eight?"

Breathe. "Like I told the other gentlemen," she explained, her impatience showing a little, "I went home." She tried not to sound curt. Didn't work. She hadn't done anything wrong and she hated being made to feel as if she had. How could this man or anyone else see her as a suspect simply because of a broken dinner date she hadn't even wanted to accept? There had to be more to it. Knowing her luck, Ned, the bastard, had screwed her one last time before getting his.

No, she decided on second thought, that wasn't it. MacBride was basing his theory on her past. *You can never outrun it.*

As if she'd telegraphed the thought straight to him, he took a step closer. She drew back a step, feeling intimidated by the idea of why he was here and somehow overwhelmed by *him.* The intensity in his eyes pressed against her, made it difficult to breathe.

"Can anyone vouch for your whereabouts?" His tone was calm, but she could feel the fierce determination beneath the innocuous words. "It would be very beneficial to you if someone could corroborate your statement."

"What's up, Elizabeth?"

Boomer planted his long lanky form right between them. She hadn't even heard him climb down from the ladder.

"Who's the suit?" His voice was calm but his body was braced for battle.

26

"It's all right," she urged in hopes of heading off any trouble for the kid. He was loyal to a fault. Always her protector, especially when they worked in rougher neighborhoods, which she'd had to do a lot of in the first few months of getting her business off the ground. He needed to steer clear on this one. "Agent MacBride is with the FBI. He has some questions about Dr. Harrison's death."

Boomer didn't appear impressed. He folded his skinny arms over his chest and continued to blatantly size up the agent. "Just let me know if he gives you any trouble. He doesn't look too friendly to me." He gave their guest a final glare before stalking back to his work.

Elizabeth almost sagged with relief. Things were bad enough without Boomer getting involved. From the unyielding expression on MacBride's face, she was pretty sure he felt nothing that even remotely resembled relief. Indifference or disapproval quite possibly, but definitely not relief.

"The answer to your question is no," she said to the agent. "I don't have anyone who can verify my whereabouts. I'm sure that was in the detectives' report. My landlady was out that night and I live alone."

Of course he knew all that, but rather than comment, he jerked his dark head in Boomer's direction. "Do you know your assistant has a significant criminal record?"

Oh, yes. Condescension, as well as disapproval. He not only knew it all, he was above it all. A blast of indignation melted some of the ice paralyzing her from the inside out. "I'm not as naive as you apparently think, Agent MacBride. I did a thorough background check before I hired him."

One dark eyebrow climbed upward a notch. "You don't mind that he's had a half-dozen drug charges, including possession with intent to sell? Or that he's done time in one of our less pleasant prison facilities?"

Rather than bank her temper, she allowed it to shore up her courage. "Everyone deserves a second chance."

He nodded knowingly, something new and primal in his eyes. "Of course. You would be a heavy supporter of second chances, wouldn't you?"

Elizabeth looked at him then, really looked at him. She no longer saw the cocky, handsome man in the thousand-dollar suit, who was perfect from the thick black hair he wore in that short, spiky style that drove women crazy all the way down to the expensive leather shoes. What she saw, instead, was a man who'd had his whole life handed to him on a silver platter. Money, the best schools, probably had never worked a day in his life until he signed on with the Bureau. And now he shined like a new penny, chasing bad guys and making the world a safer place. A hero...who didn't know the first thing about what it was like to be down on his luck.

Guys like him didn't need second chances. His world was perfect. He probably worked murder cases just to keep life interesting.

"I'm not ashamed of my past, Agent MacBride. I did what I had to do."

"I see."

She didn't miss the effort it took for him to keep a patronizing smile off his face. "Sure you do." He had no idea what her life had been like, and he sure didn't know how she felt. "How could you possibly have a clue?" She was the one who sounded condescending now.

"Of course the drugs weren't really *yours,*" he suggested, a bitter edge to his words. "But then, are they ever when an addict gets caught?" He smiled knowingly and it wasn't amusing or charming. "Taking a butcher knife to your brother-in-law was no doubt a case of self-defense. Am I right, Miss Young?"

A new burst of fury flamed inside her. She would not justify herself to this man. She'd done this song and dance twice already. He knew *nothing* about her. "Golly, mister, you must be psychic. How else could you read my mind so well? Or maybe you've got a crystal ball in your pocket."

He leaned toward her, the briefest flicker of anger in his eyes before he reined it in. "Did Harrison do something that made you take that dagger to him?" he murmured. "Were you about to be dumped *again?*"

His voice, his posture, warned he was not nearly as calm as he wanted her to believe. She held her ground, resisting the urge to flee. "I went home when he didn't show," she repeated, emphasizing each word and praying he wouldn't see the lie in her eyes. Before good sense stopped her, she tacked on, "And, for your information, I stopped seeing him weeks ago."

He leaned closer still. Her breath caught. His nostrils flared. "As a patient or as a lover?"

His cold tone made her want to draw away. Her lungs refused to draw in another breath. That clean, masculine scent had invaded her lungs and, combined with his accusation, sent her off balance. How could he know unless he'd seen the video? Her heart banged painfully against her sternum. *No one knew.* No one but Gloria, and she would never tell. Maybe he was guessing. "We weren't—" she said but he cut her off with a slow shake of his head.

"Don't lie to me, Elizabeth," he warned, the use of her first name only adding to the unbearable tension humming between them. "I've seen the video."

She stumbled back, barely missing her freshly painted wall in her effort to get away from the words she hadn't wanted to hear. Oh, God. Ned had promised to give her the video. *That night.* At dinner. He had claimed he was sorry. He hadn't meant to hurt her—he'd really liked her. He swore that he would make it up to her. But he'd lied. He refused to give her the video, and then…

She blinked back the tears stinging her eyes. She had believed him one last time and he'd lied to her. Now this man knew. He'd seen her.

As if he actually could read her mind, that relentless gaze traveled slowly down her body and, in spite of everything, heat stirred deep inside her.

Damn her traitorous body! Her pulse reacted as he retraced that path, and then looked directly into her eyes once more. "You can't hide from me, Elizabeth. I'm very good at what I do. You don't want me for an enemy."

"I'd like you to leave now, Agent MacBride." Her voice sounded oddly devoid of emotion and far steadier than she'd believed possible. She had to think. She had to talk to Gloria. Probably needed a lawyer.

"Have it your way." He reached into his pocket.

She gasped.

A grin tugged at one corner of his mouth. "Don't worry, Elizabeth. I've never shot a suspect who didn't shoot at me first."

The urge to slap that smug expression from his face was almost more than she could restrain. He handed her a business card.

"I'll see you in my office at five. *Today*. Don't be late."

Before she could argue, he turned and strode away. She watched, stunned, until he'd left the loft. She stared down at the card. Her hand shook.

This couldn't be happening. Not again.

Her heart thundered and her body flooded with adrenaline.

She couldn't breathe. Oh, God.

The trembling that had started in her hands quaked through her suddenly unsteady legs. She closed her eyes, took a long, deep breath, and let it out to the count of ten. *Breathe. Slow. Deep.* She hadn't suffered a panic attack since her third session with Ned. At least he'd been good for something.

Then he'd seduced her. Elizabeth forced her eyes open and banished those painful memories. She had to move, had to walk off the excess adrenaline.

Back and forth. Back and forth. From one end of the loft to the other. Boomer probably thought she'd lost her mind, but he didn't say anything—just did his job. *Breathe in…hold it…breathe out. Again.*

Ned had taken advantage of her. He had used her. Now he was dead and it looked as if he was taking her down with him. Why hadn't she stayed until he'd given her the video? She should have done whatever he asked—anything for the video. But no, she'd stormed off, knowing she'd have no choice but to go crawling back when he called again. She'd been angry.

She'd had no idea she would never see him alive again.

Mac braked to a stop in the empty street. His gaze drifted up to the fourth floor where he'd left Elizabeth. He pounded the steering wheel. He'd done a bang-up job of recovering the ground the detectives had lost. He called himself every kind of fool. Cool, he was supposed to have played it cool. Give her space, let her tell her story. Gently guide her as necessary.

Damn.

He'd failed on all counts. If he could have kicked himself in the ass, he would have. His body hummed with anticipation. He gritted his teeth and denied the other sensation sparring with her had elicited. It was that very reaction that made him push harder than he'd intended. He'd shaken her. The hell of it was, he was just as rattled.

He hissed a disgusted breath.

By five o'clock when she arrived at his office, and she would come, she'd have an attorney at her side. Then he would get nowhere even faster. He had to find a way to regain some of the ground he'd lost.

His attention settled on a dark sedan parked on the opposite side of the street in a neighboring alley. Just in case the lady decided to cut her losses and make a run for it, someone would be watching.

His cell rang at the same time a horn blared behind him. Mac pressed the accelerator and started forward while retrieving his phone.

"MacBride."

"You're going to love this."

Duncan. "What've you got?"

"We traced the dagger to an antique shop over on West Fifty-fifth."

"Yeah." There was more. He heard it in his partner's voice. Mac felt a new kind of anticipation spike.

"It was purchased as a gift for Harrison by Miss Elizabeth Young."

Mac's tension eased marginally at the news that at least one loose end was tied up. "Good work." He ignored an uncharacteristic twinge of regret that followed close behind the relief. She'd already lied to him so he shouldn't be surprised by this latest development. Yet he was. She'd gotten to him on some level. He didn't like it. Not in the least. "See you in thirty," he told his partner.

The news would certainly work to his advantage. He couldn't wait to see how Elizabeth planned to talk her way out of this one. He shook his head as he thought of the pretty lady who could win herself an Oscar for her portrayal of innocence and suffering.

"Gotcha," he muttered.

CHAPTER THREE

Elizabeth waited in Chico's Cantina. She pressed a hand to her knee to stop her foot's tapping. She rolled her head side to side to relieve some of the tension in her neck. Didn't help.

One-fifteen. Gloria was late. Elizabeth let go an unsteady breath and fiddled with the straw in her cola. She had to get hold of herself. She couldn't let MacBride get to her this way. He'd been worse than those two detectives put together. Something was different about him. More intimidating. A subtle ruthlessness that frightened her. This was a man who wouldn't give up until he knew everything.

She hadn't done anything wrong. Sure, there'd been moments when Ned's actions had made her want to kill him, but she hadn't. Thinking about it wasn't against the law. Probably dozens of women, especially former patients, had thought about it more than once.

Maybe one of them had actually done it.

Elizabeth went rigid. Could one of the women who'd come to his funeral have been his killer? Was that why MacBride had been in attendance?

He suspected *her.* That was the reason he'd put in an appearance. Something frigid seeped into her bones. He'd discovered the video of her and Ned and he'd put it together with the dinner date on Ned's calendar and come up with murder. She sipped her cola to wet her desperately dry throat. How long would it be before he found out about the two huge arguments they'd had? Very public arguments, one in the lobby of Ned's office and another at that party. She'd slapped him during the second one. He'd grabbed her by the shoulders and shaken her and she'd slapped him again.

And she'd…God, she'd told him he would be sorry. Had anyone heard her rant? She'd made a threat against him, there was no other way to interpret the words, but she hadn't really meant it. Everyone said things like that in the heat of anger. She wouldn't be the first or the last—except maybe where Ned Harrison was concerned.

Had she been the last person to threaten him out loud? In front of dozens of witnesses?

Elizabeth pressed a hand to her lips and closed her eyes long enough to pull herself together. The evidence would be stacked against her. She was an outsider. It would be much easier and certainly less messy to pin the rap on her. She could barely afford her rent at the moment. A high priced attorney was out of the question. If she was stuck in a jail cell, she'd lose her contract on the rest of the lofts and any prospects of future income.

She had no family who could help. Her sister, Peg, would sympathize, but it was all she could do to keep a roof over her three kids' heads. Too bad that scumbag she'd been married to hadn't had any life insurance. Then when he'd careened off a bridge and into a river while intoxicated, at least he would have been worth something. Instead, her sister had struggled to scrape together the money to bury the worthless scumbag.

Elizabeth swiped her eyes and forced herself to think calmly. She wasn't guilty. Surely the real murderer had left some sort of evidence. She knew Ned had been with someone else that night. It was why he hadn't shown for their dinner date. Had that woman returned later and killed him, or was it someone else entirely? Maybe she'd even been hiding in the apartment while Elizabeth was there. She had thought he was alone when she confronted him, but someone had definitely been there shortly before her abrupt arrival. She'd seen the tousled sheets, smelled the musky scent of sex.

The son of a bitch.

She drew in a deep breath and again focused on calming her racing heart and jangled nerves. When she'd left Ned Harrison he had been very much alive. MacBride would never believe her. If she admitted she'd gone to Ned's apartment, he would use it against her. Besides, she was pretty sure no one had seen her. Why give the authorities any more ammunition than they already had? She'd be a fool not to recognize she was at the top of the suspect list already.

She couldn't tell MacBride anything and risk being charged with Ned's murder. The truth didn't always set you free. Elizabeth had learned that lesson long ago.

The bell above the door jingled, drawing her back to the here and now. Gloria stopped just inside the entrance and scanned the small cantina. Elizabeth waved and her friend rushed over, a brief-case-size purse hanging on one shoulder, a folded newspaper tucked under the opposite arm.

"Sorry I'm late." She dropped into the seat across from Elizabeth. "Last-minute BS on an hour long conference call that shouldn't have lasted more than five minutes." She beamed a smile and lifted one eyebrow triumphantly. "But I saved the account. Everyone, including Murphy, was suitably impressed."

Murphy was Gloria's boss. She continually surprised the man. Gloria insisted it was the luck of the Irish. Elizabeth knew differently. Her friend was smart and relentless, and had a sixth sense about market maneuvers. Those stubborn Irish genes didn't hurt.

Wriggling out of her elegant suit jacket, Gloria called out her drink order to the passing waitress.

Elizabeth smiled for the first time that day. One of the things she liked most about Chico's was that everyone was treated the same. It didn't matter if you arrived wearing a power suit or baggy denim overalls. People from all walks of life frequented the place. Elizabeth could look around right now and point out the stock traders like her friend, the computer geeks, the starving artists and the electricians and plumbers who were much like her. No one, particularly the cantina staff, seemed to pay any attention to the differences.

"Sounds like your day was better than mine," Elizabeth commented thinly, thoughts of MacBride's visit drawing the black clouds low over her head.

Gloria studied her closely as the waitress plunked her diet soda before her. "You look like someone under bid you on a big contract. What happened?"

Elizabeth clutched her hands together in her lap and swore she would not get emotional. She had to stay calm. "An FBI agent paid me a visit today."

Surprise claimed her friend's features. "An *FBI* agent?"

Elizabeth nodded. "You remember after the funeral I told you about the good-looking guy who'd been so nice to me? You know, he gave me his handkerchief, like guys in the old movies we watch?"

A predatory gleam flashed in Gloria's eyes. "Oh, yeah. You said he was really something."

Elizabeth nodded grimly. "He is. He's an FBI agent and he was there watching me."

Disbelief registered. "He told you that?"

Elizabeth shrugged. "In a roundabout way."

Gloria shook her head. "This is insane. How could they suspect you?"

Elizabeth stared at the red-and-white checked tablecloth. God, she didn't want to have to tell Gloria this. The subject was still a little tender between them. Summoning her determination, Elizabeth lifted her gaze to her friend's and confessed, "He asked me to have dinner with him…the night of his murder."

A beat of silence echoed, blocking out all other sound.

"Ned asked you to have dinner with him?" The color of excitement that had tinged Gloria's cheeks only moments ago paled. "You didn't agree. Not after…"

Her words trailed off. She didn't have to say the rest. Elizabeth knew.

Dammit, she knew.

She blinked back the tears she'd sworn she wouldn't allow to fall. "He said he'd give me the video."

"The video?" A stillness settled over Gloria.

Elizabeth nodded. "He promised he'd give it to me if I'd have dinner with him." There was no need to tell her the rest. Ned had hurt them both badly enough. She wasn't about to add insult to injury by telling Gloria he'd gone on and on about how much he cared for Elizabeth. It was all lies anyway.

A line of confusion or maybe irritation creased Gloria's usually smooth brow. "And you believed him?"

"I was afraid," she confessed, her voice wavered. "I didn't know what he'd do with it if I didn't take it when he offered. There's no telling what he might've done if—"

"You're not the only woman he videoed," Gloria said bluntly, all emotion except one—desperation—visibly draining from her. "He probably had one on each of us."

"Maybe he destroyed the others," Elizabeth offered, but they both knew that wasn't likely.

Gloria snorted a dry laugh as she shook her head, her gaze distant, no longer focused on Elizabeth. "That lowlife bastard. I should have known he couldn't be trusted."

Elizabeth frowned. "How could you have known?"

Gloria gave a start, as if she'd forgotten where she was. She seemed suddenly out of sorts. "No, no. I...I meant that neither of us should be surprised by anything the cops uncover about him."

"That's true." Elizabeth didn't have time to analyze Gloria's sudden edginess before they were interrupted.

"You ladies ready to order now?" The waitress paused at their table, the pencil in her hand poised above her pad.

Gloria ordered her usual salad with dressing on the side. Elizabeth ordered the same, since she wasn't very hungry. When the waitress moved on, Gloria propped her elbows on the table and focused on Elizabeth.

"All right, so tell me what the fed wanted."

Elizabeth wrapped her arms around herself, feeling cold and oddly alone. "He wants to prove I killed Ned."

"But you didn't kill Ned," Gloria countered, the edge back in her voice. "He can't pin anything on you without evidence."

"He knows we were supposed to have dinner that night." Elizabeth resisted the urge to look away. This was Gloria. Her best friend in the whole world, no matter what had gone down between them where Ned was concerned. Elizabeth could trust Gloria.

"Did you have dinner together?" she asked pointedly, her eyes giving away the hurt hovering just beneath her strained composure.

"I went. For the video," Elizabeth added emphatically. "He didn't show. I waited about an hour and then I left."

"Someone at the restaurant saw you, I presume."

Elizabeth nodded. She sat up straighter, feeling suddenly ill at ease with the tone of Gloria's voice. What was the deal here? Was Gloria upset about Ned calling her? Elizabeth had thought they were past all this. They had both been fooled by the man. After much shouting and many tears they'd reached an understanding…and put it behind them.

Until now, it seemed.

Damn him. If Ned had to die, why didn't he just do it the old-fashioned way? A simple heart attack. Or, hell, even a taxi accident. Lord knew the cab drivers in this city were more than a little reckless.

"You told the fed that he didn't show and that you went home, right?"

"Yes, but I don't think he believed me."

A new wariness slipped into Gloria's strangely unsympathetic expression. "Why wouldn't he believe you?"

Elizabeth's heart threatened to burst from her chest. She wet her lips and forced out the words she didn't want to say. "Because I lied."

Gloria huffed in disbelief. "Damn it, Elizabeth, why did you do that?"

"I was angry, okay?" The people at the next table turned and stared. Elizabeth took a breath and ordered herself to be calm once more, then began again, quietly, for Gloria's ears only. "I wanted him to know he should never call me again. I was tired of him hurting us. So I went to his apartment. I banged on the door until he answered." She shook her head. "He was pulling his clothes on, insisting he was running late." She clenched her jaw to slow the emotions mounting all over again. "I knew he was lying."

"What'd you do?"

"I stormed into the apartment and straight to the bedroom. The sheets were tousled." Her gaze locked with Gloria's. "He'd called and pleaded with me to meet him for dinner, then kept me waiting an entire hour while he had a romp in the sack with someone else."

Gloria closed her eyes and shuddered visibly. "Bastard," she hissed. "I'm glad he's dead."

Elizabeth scrubbed her hands over her face. "We argued. I told him never to call me again and then I demanded the video." She made a sound, something along the lines of a laugh, but pathetically lacking in humor. "He just laughed at me. He…" She chewed her lower lip to stem the tears threatening. "He was going to use it to blackmail me. He told me I'd get it when he was through with me." She shrugged, still scarcely believing her own stupidity. "I couldn't believe it."

Gloria's breathing had grown as rapid and as shallow as Elizabeth's. "Tell me exactly what you did then."

"I slapped him and he…he tried to…" She frowned, trying to remember the exact sequence of events. "He grabbed my arm and I fought to get away. Then I ran out."

"Okay," Gloria said, noticeably grappling for her own composure. "You listen to me, Elizabeth. You do exactly as I say. Do you hear me?"

She nodded.

Gloria released a shaky breath. "You stick to your original story. He didn't show, you went home. Don't tell the cops anything else. This is a high-profile case. They'll want to solve it as soon as possible. Pinning the rap on you would be the fastest route." She reached across the table and placed a reassuring hand over Elizabeth's. "What about the video?"

God, she could just die. "That's the worst part. He wouldn't give it to me…and the cops found it. That FBI agent, MacBride, told me he'd viewed it."

"Oh hell."

"My sentiments exactly." Elizabeth stared down at their hands. What a mess. She might as well face it. She was in serious trouble.

"Look." Gloria drew Elizabeth's gaze back to hers. "You didn't kill him. They can't prove you did. Having sex with a man doesn't make you guilty of murder."

Elizabeth managed a shaky smile. Her friend was right. Regardless of how it looked, she was innocent.

"True," she agreed. She studied Gloria for a long moment trying to see what it was that nagged at her. She supposed her friend was just afraid for her... or angry that Ned had once again hurt her. "I really didn't kill him, you know."

Gloria squeezed her hand. "I know you didn't. The cops are just looking for an easy out. If they had any real evidence, they'd arrest you."

Been there, done that, bought the t-shirt, Elizabeth thought grimly. "The agent brought up Billy and the drug charge."

Gloria knew the whole sordid story about Billy, the brother-in-law from hell, and the time Elizabeth had claimed her sister's drug stash to save her from a beating. Elizabeth had never even tried drugs, but she had a possession charge on her record because she'd gone the distance for her only sibling. The other incident had been ruled self-defense. Peg was pregnant with her third child and her stupid husband had come home in a drunken rage and started beating her. Expecting to go into labor at any time, Elizabeth had spent the night at her sister's since Billy was rarely around. Something had snapped inside her that night as she'd witnessed him beating her very pregnant sister. He'd come after her and Elizabeth had stopped him with the only weapon in the house, a butcher knife. She hadn't killed him but she'd wanted to...she would have done anything to make him stop.

"Well," Gloria said, dragging Elizabeth from the past, "that still doesn't make you a murderer."

Elizabeth wrapped her arms around herself again. "No, but it puts me at the top of the suspect list."

Gloria frowned suddenly, as if she'd just remembered something important. "You said this MacBride is from the FBI?"

Elizabeth nodded.

"Why would the FBI investigate a simple homicide case?"

"They must think his murder is connected to others or," she turned her hands up, "to some criminal activity where the feds have jurisdiction."

"Or maybe we've just seen too many TV dramas," Gloria teased, acting more like her old self now. "Maybe the cops asked for their help since it's such a high-profile case. The media is all over every aspect of the investigation."

"I guess so." Another thought occurred to Elizabeth. She shook her head in frustration. "It would be just my luck they think I'm some sort of serial killer."

Gloria pressed her hand to her chest "Speaking of murder, I almost forgot" She grabbed the newspaper she'd tossed on the bench seat next to her. "Look at this." She spread it open on the table.

She pointed to a headline that read *Fashion Designer Found Murdered.* Elizabeth skimmed the brief article. The details were gruesome.

"Remember her?"

Elizabeth glanced from the unnerving article to her friend. "Should I?"

"Look at the picture." She tapped the photo to the left of the article.

Recognition dawned. The long-legged, raven-haired beauty at the funeral. The one with the Johnny Depp lookalike for an escort. "Oh, my God." She looked up at Gloria. "She sat a couple rows in front of us at the funeral."

Gloria nodded. "The scuttlebutt is that someone in the industry did in the hottest new competition."

"My God," Elizabeth repeated. She stared at the article. Who gave the press permission to print such grim specifics? Weren't those details supposed to be kept hush-hush? The woman's body had been found in her bedroom. Her throat had been slashed. "What kind of person could do that to another human being?"

"Yeah, really." Gloria tapped the newspaper. "That's the murder the cops and your FBI friend should be investigating. Not wasting time on some bastard who only got what he deserved."

Elizabeth refolded the paper so she wouldn't have to look at the woman's picture. It was definitely too much right before lunch. "I'll be sure to tell him that at our five o'clock meeting."

Gloria tensed. "You have to talk to him again today?"

Elizabeth nodded. "At his office." Seeing Gloria's gaping expression, she added, "I think he's trying to intimidate me into a confession."

"Don't tell him anything he doesn't need to know," Gloria warned again. "In fact, I'll talk to a friend of mine about a good attorney for you, if you'd like."

A worried sigh escaped Elizabeth. "I hope it doesn't come to that."

"I don't think it will." Gloria sounded a lot more confident than Elizabeth felt. "But it would be nice to have the right name to toss around. It might even get the feds off your back."

"Good idea."

The waitress zipped by, pausing long enough to deposit their salads and to ask if they needed anything else. They both replied no.

Elizabeth dribbled ranch dressing over her salad, noting that Gloria did not. Her friend was extremely calorie-conscious. Elizabeth supposed it paid to be when you spent twelve hours a day behind a desk. Gloria had made the comment on several occasions that the asses of her female coworkers got wider every day. Gloria had no intention of following that trend. The one good thing about Elizabeth's line of work was that she got plenty of exercise.

She smacked her forehead with the heel of her hand. She'd almost forgotten again. "How's your niece?"

Gloria appeared taken aback by the question. "She's fine. Why do you ask?"

"You mentioned she was having some trouble a couple of months ago, and I keep forgetting to ask how she's doing." Gloria seemed put off by the subject. The two of them usually talked about everything. Her niece, apparently, was as touchy a subject as Ned.

"You know how it is when you're eighteen and a freshman in college," Gloria said dismissively. "You think nobody knows anything but you. Since her father's death last year, she's sort of withdrawn from everyone, especially her mother. It hasn't been easy, but she's managing."

Elizabeth remembered that terrible night Gloria had called. Her brother-in-law, an NYPD fireman, had been killed in the line of duty. His wife and daughter were devastated. Not long after that, Elizabeth's father had died. God, that had been a lousy month.

"I'm glad she's doing better," Elizabeth said, feeling bad for bringing up the subject, yet knowing she'd feel guilty if she hadn't. "It's tough to lose your father, especially at that age." At any age, Elizabeth thought. She still missed hers.

Gloria picked at her salad. "She's all my sister has left." Her tone was somber. "We have to protect her at all costs."

Elizabeth paused, a forkful of salad halfway to her mouth. Her friend's swift mood changes were disturbing. So unlike Gloria. "Of course you have to protect her," Elizabeth agreed gently. "Let me know if there's anything I can do to help."

Gloria smiled, but the expression didn't reach her eyes. "Just keep me up-to-date on what's going on with your fed." Her faint smile widened to a genuine grin. "And remember, if things get too hairy, you can always seduce him."

Elizabeth almost choked on a cherry tomato. "Yeah, right," she muttered when she'd stopped coughing. "I don't think MacBride is seducible." She remembered vividly his steely gaze and precisely controlled responses. He wasn't the kind of man a simple girl like her could get to…even if she wanted to.

"Oh, honey, that's the country girl in you talking," Gloria scolded, the words and the tone so very Gloria. "They're *all* seducible. Trust me."

"I'll bear that in mind." Elizabeth refused to analyze the warm glow that accompanied the ridiculous suggestion. Gloria had no business putting ideas like that in her head. An affair with another man she couldn't trust was the last thing Elizabeth needed. Especially since this one suspected her of murder.

And had seen her naked having sex with another man.

How would she ever face MacBride this afternoon?

CHAPTER FOUR

"I'll have to see your ID, sir," the uniform posted in the entry hall of the penthouse announced as Mac stepped off the elevator.

It wasn't as if he hadn't flashed his ID in the lobby before he boarded the only elevator in the building that went all the way to the top floor. Rather than informing the rookie of that, Mac fished in his pocket for his badge and showed it again.

The uniform, whose badge read Ledbetter, flushed. "Sorry, sir, but a reporter managed to get inside last night before the homicide detectives got here and we've all been instructed to double-check IDs."

"No problem." Mac ducked beneath the police tape that marked the penthouse apartment off-limits to anyone other than authorized NYPD personnel. He hadn't needed Officer Ledbetter to tell him the perimeter had been breached sometime shortly after the discovery of the body. The morning's headlines had shouted that loud and clear. It only made bad matters worse that the breach had occurred before the arrival of the crime-scene techs. There was no telling what the eager reporter had contaminated in his haste to get the story.

Mac paused long enough in the doorway to slip on gloves and paper shoe covers. As he prepped for entering the crime scene, he noted the fingerprint powder on the handles of the elegant double doors separating the posh Upper Eastside penthouse from the entry hall. It would take days if not weeks for the techs to sort through all the prints lifted from a place this size. The socialite who owned the place had a reputation for hosting grand parties. Most of Manhattan's upper crust likely waltzed through these doors at one time or another.

The whish-whish of paper shoe covers echoed from farther down the hall. Mac surveyed his surroundings as he made his way in the direction of the sound. A grand dining room and great room flanked the hall on either side a few feet beyond the main doors. A small powder room and guest bedroom lay on the right beyond the formal rooms, then the hall took a slight turn to the left and opened up into an extravagantly appointed sitting area that bordered a massive master suite.

This was where the murder had taken place.

Mac paused, his gaze landing on the spray of blood fanned across the wall above the headboard. No matter how many crime scenes he'd examined in his ten-year career, the initial sight of spilled blood always shook him. The victim would already be in the capable hands of the medical examiner, but telltale signs of the final battle for life she'd waged were clear to all who entered this room.

Through the floor-to-ceiling windows, which displayed a magnificent Manhattan view, brilliant sunlight poured into the room, gleaming on the plush, sand-colored carpet. Despite the two techs working vigorously, collecting everything from fibers on the carpeted floor to dust on the glittering chandelier, the room felt vast and empty. The stark white walls framing the space were marred only by the blood that had trickled down like garish streamers toward the rumpled bed.

Judging by the blood spatter pattern the victim had been dragged from the bed for the final affront levied by the intruder. The tousled condition of the silk and satin covers indicated she hadn't been in bed alone. He thought about the undamaged doors, handles and lock assembly he'd viewed while slipping on his gloves and shoe covers and decided that *intruder* wasn't the right word. Whoever had done this had been allowed—if not invited—in by the victim. Since the front doors were the only means of entry, windows were not a likely avenue considering they were on the thirtieth floor, he had to assume the victim knew her killer.

The bloody tracks on the carpet indicated the unknown subject had left his dying victim and walked to the en suite for a shower before leaving.

"Agent MacBride?"

Mac turned to the familiar voice coming from the doorway behind him and bit back a curse.

Detective Brannigan. The last person he wanted to see. He hoped like hell the guy wasn't the lead on this homicide, too. He enjoyed giving Mac a hard time entirely too much. Mac got it. No one liked having another agency horn in on a case, even if the order to play nice came from the top brass. The detective needn't worry, Mac had no desire to get in NYPD's way on these homicides. His goal was to find the link to the Gentlemen's Association.

"Officer Ledbetter told me you were here." Brannigan glanced at the bloody wall as he moved into the room. "I'm lead on this investigation. What interest do you have in this case? Surely the Federal Bureau of Investigation has other things to do besides nosing into my cases."

Damn.

Brannigan resented like hell that Mac was involved with the Harrison case. He wasn't going to be happy about him showing up here.

"Vanessa Bumbalough was one of Harrison's patients. She also attended his funeral." Mac surveyed the enormous room once more. The techs had paused in their work to listen to the exchange.

"That's correct," Brannigan said. The fury that simmered in his eyes belied his even tone. "But I can't see how those details tie into her murder."

Mac thought about the condition of the room. The overturned bedside table, the twisted bedcovers, the blood. Then he considered the rest of what he'd seen in the grand penthouse—immaculate, every little thing in place. The victim had known the unsub, no question. During the lull the techs turned their attention back to the task of collecting any evidence they'd missed on their first sweep, which likely took place late last night after the discovery of the body.

"Were there any witnesses?" Mac asked rather than responding to Brannigan's comment regarding the victim's connection, or lack thereof, with Harrison.

The middle-aged detective shook his head. "No one saw or heard anything. The doorman insists no one other than residents entered the building yesterday. He checked the log."

"I assume there was more than one doorman during the twenty-four hours prior to the body's discovery."

Brannigan shoved his hands into his trouser pockets. "There were four and we interviewed all of 'em. Doormen and anyone else who worked on the premises in the last forty-eight hours."

"The other residents?"

"We're working on that right now. It takes time to cover this many apartments."

"Of course."

"We're also talking to the people she worked with," Brannigan went on as if he felt the need to prove himself. "With all the hoopla surrounding her splash onto the fashion scene, it could've been a competitor."

Mac looked around the room again. "Maybe."

"And maybe it was a jealous lover," Brannigan said in a tone just shy of seething. "We're still looking for the guy who accompanied her to Harrison's funeral. From what we've learned, she recently dumped her longtime lover for him. We haven't located the jilted lover, either, but we will."

Mac nodded, affirming the detective's conclusions. "That would be the most logical avenue to follow."

Brannigan shifted his considerable bulk from one foot to the other. "I suppose you want details about the murder."

Mac lifted a skeptical eyebrow. "Are there any that weren't in the newspaper this morning?"

Brannigan's hostile retort snagged the attention of everyone in the room. He glared at the techs, who immediately returned to the task at hand. "We got that little mystery solved," he grumbled, a bit more courteously. "One of our new guys has a cousin who's a reporter. That won't happen again."

Vanessa Bumbalough had been found in a skimpy negligee, tied to her bed and with her throat slashed. All that information had been in the paper.

"There was one thing," Brannigan said after a moment and with obvious reluctance.

Mac waited, trying not to let his exasperation show. Brannigan would give him the details in his own time and Mac would drum up as much patience as necessary. One way or another he was bringing the Gentlemen's Association down. Ned Harrison and anyone related to his life and death could prove relevant to that end.

"The reporter didn't get a chance to see *this*," Brannigan explained smugly, "before he was ousted."

"What would *this* be?" Mac asked when the detective hesitated for the dramatic effect.

"The victim was gagged—with a pair of panties."

Mac went on alert. Harrison had a pair of panties shoved into his mouth to silence him—one of the view details not leaked to the press. Frustration and no small amount of anger twisted Mac's gut. "With the vic's link to Harrison you didn't feel the need to pass this information along before now?" Hell, he wouldn't even be here if he hadn't read this morning's paper.

"The size and brand suggest they belonged to the vic. There's a whole drawer full just like'em," Brannigan said, ignoring his question. He rocked back on his heels, seemingly pleased that Mac was pissed. "The killer shoved them so far back in her throat she'd have choked to death even if he hadn't slit her throat."

"What makes you think the killer is male?" There was more. Mac could feel it. Brannigan's whole demeanor was far too cocky. It was fairly obvious the victim, like Harrison, had engaged in sexual activity prior to her death. Had the ME confirmed?

The detective shrugged nonchalantly. "The ME mentioned he thought the victim had been sexually assaulted but wouldn't confirm. She had sex, we just don't know if it was consensual."

When Mac had gleaned all he could from the scene and tolerated all of Brannigan's gloating he could stomach, he made his way back to the elevator and down to the lobby. He checked his cell as he settled behind the wheel of his sedan. He still had time to drop by the morgue and take a look at the body before the meeting with Elizabeth Young.

If, as Brannigan suggested, Bumbalough had been sexually assaulted, he wanted to know details. Had she first consented, then changed her mind? Or was the act a flat-out rape from the get-go? If she hadn't resisted, that would lend credence to the idea that she knew her attacker.

One thing was certain, if the victim's killer was male and there was a connection to Harrison's murder that could very well let Elizabeth Young off the hook.

Mac guided his sedan into the flow of traffic and thought about that scenario for a moment. Maybe it wouldn't let her off the hook. Maybe she and the killer were a team. Of course, connecting Harrison's murder with this one, even though the victim was one of his patients and had attended his funeral, was a stretch. Except for the panties.

Could be coincidence. But Mac's instincts were humming. He had a feeling the two were connected. He mentally ran through the similarities. The victims had been restrained, both had been gagged with panties, and now there was the possibility that both had participated in sexual activity prior to death.

Coincidences? Maybe.

Too soon to tell. But he would find out. Because whether Brannigan liked it or not, Mac wouldn't let it go until he knew for certain whether the two cases were connected.

Elizabeth stood outside the FBI Office and took a deep breath. She had to do this. Had to be calm and collected, as well as strong. She'd left work early this afternoon and gone home long enough to change into the one and only suit she owned. A black pencil skirt and matching single-breasted jacket. It was the lone remaining ensemble from her days with Brian and the firm. Everything else she'd burned in a bonfire one night after too much wine with Gloria. She'd learned very quickly that even in a not-so-upscale neighborhood people called the police when they saw suspicious activity.

She'd almost gotten arrested for the act of liberation. Ultimately the cop had felt sorry for her since she'd just been dumped and lost her job on the same day. So he'd ushered her and Gloria back into her apartment and made them swear they would sleep it off before undertaking any other activities. The next morning she'd awakened with the kind of headache one got from drinking too much wine and with a closet that was considerably emptier. She suddenly wished she could go back to that night, or at least the morning after. That was the morning she'd made the decision to go see the shrink Gloria had recommended for the panic attacks she'd suffered for nearly a year. That decision had led her to this place.

Elizabeth braced herself for the worst and entered the intimidating building.

After consulting a directory she crossed the cavernous lobby and hesitated at the security checkpoint.

"I'll need a picture ID, ma'am," the guard informed her. "Place your purse here." He indicated the small conveyor belt that reminded her of the larger ones at airports.

She dug out her driver's license and held it up for his inspection then handed over her bag for inspection. "I have a five o'clock appointment with Agent Collin MacBride."

The guard checked his list and then nodded for her to pass through the metal detector. On the other side, he returned her purse. Elizabeth thanked him and tucked away her license. Once at the elevator she smoothed a hand over her jacket and pressed the call button. The doors slid open immediately and the moment she selected the proper floor the doors closed and she was whisked upward.

The blue-carpeted reception area on the twenty-seventh floor was sparsely furnished and unembellished except for the enormous FBI seal decorating the far wall. The seal boasted of pride and demanded respect and managed to undo every scrap of bravado Elizabeth had mustered.

She moistened her lips and held on to the shoulder strap of her purse. Might as well get this over with. She strode to the receptionist's desk. "Hello, I'm—"

"Miss Young?"

The voice jerked her around as efficiently as if its owner had grabbed her by the arm and pulled.

"I'm Agent Luke Duncan," the man said "We've been waiting for you. If you'll come this way please."

Blood roaring in her ears, Elizabeth allowed Agent Duncan to direct her down a long corridor to the sixth office on the right. He opened the door and stood back for her to enter ahead of him.

Elizabeth studied his face for a moment before she did so, but she found no comfort, no assurance that all would come out right. She was on her own here. She should have listened to Gloria and called that attorney. But she couldn't afford a fancy Manhattan attorney. If she could get this matter straightened out without having to go into hock for a retainer, she would.

Forcing one foot in front of the other, she walked into the office and Duncan closed the door behind her. She glanced over her shoulder and wasn't surprised to find that he hadn't followed her inside.

Left alone in Agent MacBride's office, Elizabeth used the time to learn what she could about the man. Graduated from Columbia University. She read each of the accolades hanging on his walls. Plaque after plaque lauding his dedication and heroics. Certificate after certificate praising his work. There were numerous pictures of him receiving commendations. But there wasn't the first sign of family or loved ones. No pictures on the desk or wall of anyone other than those related to work. Nothing.

Like the man, the office was elegant. She wondered if all FBI agents had mahogany desks and credenzas, expensive leather upholstered chairs and a view looking out over the city he served and protected. Somehow she doubted it. These luxuries were probably his personal belongings. They matched his thousand-dollar suits and Italian-made shoes.

She wondered what kind of house he lived in and just how much an FBI agent was paid. Not this much, she'd bet. Collin MacBride was exactly what she'd suspected—a rich guy with a need to prove his worth. She surveyed the many plaques and pictures that attested to his accomplishments. Just what she needed. A refined greyhound with the simpleminded tenacity of a pit bull.

The door opened and she turned as Agent MacBride entered his office. The air felt suddenly charged, and the room instantly seemed to shrink to half its size. Fear coiled around her chest, tightening until she could scarcely breathe.

"Miss Young, I apologize for keeping you waiting." He skirted his desk and gestured to one of the chairs waiting on her side.

She sat, tried to moisten her lips, but her mouth was too dry to make a difference. The pounding in her chest was almost deafening. She forced herself to focus on the man as he opened a file on his desk and appeared to review the contents.

He was tall and just as handsome and well dressed as she remembered. A thin swirl of heat chased away some of the chill she'd experienced from the moment she entered the building. A frown nagged at her forehead as she tried to analyze the ridiculous reaction. She needed to lay off the power drinks. Like caffeine was the reason for her hot flashes in this guy's presence. Ha. Before she admitted the surge of heat for what it was, he spoke again.

"Have you thought about our earlier visit?" he asked in that smooth voice that spoke of breeding and an Ivy League education.

Had she thought about it? Fury seared away all other emotion. What did he think? "Actually," she said, not bothering to keep the outrage out of her tone and lying through her teeth, "I haven't had time to think about anything but work. Was there something in particular I should have thought about?"

He smiled, but it was not understanding or even polite. "Do you recognize this?" He tossed a photograph to her side of the desk.

Gingerly she reached for it. Her breath stalled in the farthest recesses of her lungs when she recognized the object pictured in the eight-by-ten print.

The dagger.

The one she'd found at the junk store on Fifty-fifth. The one she'd bought Ned as a thank-you for helping her with her panic attacks. The gift she'd given him before she'd recognized him for the monster he was.

"I thought you might," MacBride said arrogantly.

Her gaze shot to his. "So what if I do?" Her words were shrouded with mounting dread. Somehow some part of her knew this was bad. Very bad. She pitched the photograph back to his side of the desk as if merely holding it would further condemn her.

"That's the murder weapon." He picked up the picture and pretended to study it. "It was buried to the hilt just left of the victim's sternum." He shook his head solemnly. "Slid right between the ribs, punctured a lung and nicked the pericardium." He shrugged then. "He couldn't have lived more than a few minutes. Not even long enough for help to arrive had someone called for it."

A wobbly sensation spread through her entire body. She stared at her fingers as if she could still them by sheer force of will, but she couldn't. Her stomach roiled and for one beat she was certain she'd be sick.

"Except no one called for help. Whoever plunged this dagger," he tapped the photo, "into Ned's chest left him there, naked and dying."

Elizabeth lifted her gaze to meet his. "I didn't do it." She struggled to swallow back some of the desperation tightening her throat. "I swear I didn't kill him."

Those blue eyes bored more deeply into hers, that relentlessness she'd recognized yesterday flashing like a neon sign. "All I want from you, Elizabeth, is the truth."

The truth.

How could she hope to fool this man?

Gloria's words echoed in her ears. *Stick with your original story. Don't tell the cops anything else.*

She drew in a ragged breath. "I've already told you everything I know."

Lights pulsed behind her eyes. Nausea burned bitter and hot in her throat. She'd never before had a migraine, but the abrupt chord of pain in her skull now was no ordinary headache.

He didn't even blink, just kept watching her. "I don't think you have, Miss Young."

Unable to sit there another second, she lurched to her feet. "I've told you everything. This…this harassment is pointless. I can't help you, Agent MacBride."

She whipped around and headed for the door. She had to get out of here. The pain was excruciating, the trembling almost violent. If she didn't leave now, she might not be able to do so under her own steam. She would not give him the pleasure of seeing her collapse beneath the pressure.

Before she could jerk the door open, he was standing next to her, one broad palm plastered against the slab of wood that stood between her and escape.

"If you think of anything you need to tell me, my cell number is on the card I gave you."

She closed her eyes and struggled to hold herself steady. "I won't think of anything." Forcing her eyes open, she met that blue gaze. "You shouldn't be wasting your time on me, Agent MacBride. You should be out there looking for the killer."

"What is it you're afraid of, Elizabeth?" he asked softly, the gentle tone a vivid contrast to the fierceness in his eyes.

Shaking her head in denial, she glared at him with all the disdain she could marshal. "I'm innocent." She'd meant to hurl the words at him with fierce determination, but she'd fallen well short of the mark. All she'd managed to do was sound desperate.

"Then you won't mind submitting to certain tests," he suggested in that same smooth baritone.

Tests? Her mind spun with the possibilities. Had she touched anything? Left prints or some form of DNA that would tighten the noose already around her neck?

She remembered slapping Ned. Maybe she'd scratched him. He'd grabbed her brutally. Shaken her. Had she lost a loose hair on his sleeve?

Her heart slammed mercilessly against her rib cage. That was it. She'd watched enough CSI episodes to realize what he was up to.

"Elizabeth? Is there a problem with my request?"

Her gaze locked with his once more and she shook her head. "Call my attorney." She rattled off the name of the legal eagle Gloria had given her. "You can discuss it with him." She couldn't take any more. Couldn't do this. Not again. Not alone.

He leaned in closer, square into her personal space. "I'll call him, Elizabeth, but that's not all I'm going to do."

She swallowed, hard. Grasped the anger that swelled just enough to give her the strength to demand, "Is that a threat?"

He smiled and her foolish heart skipped a beat. This close she could feel the pleasure it gave him to have her trapped so firmly in his net of suspicion. She wanted to pound on that broad chest of his and rant at him. She wanted to shake him until he realized she was telling the truth. She did not kill Ned Harrison. She was innocent. Why couldn't he see that?

But she couldn't do any of those things. All she could do was stare into those intense eyes and fight the urge to admit defeat.

"No threat" he said on something that could have been a sigh but sounded more like a scoff. "Just fair warning." All signs of amusement or gentleness vanished then. That chiseled jaw hardened like granite. "I'll be watching you, Elizabeth. If you make one mistake, I'll know it." The corners of those firm lips tilted upward, hinted at a smile. "And you will make a mistake. They all do."

For two long beats she stood frozen, staring into those accusing eyes, and then he moved. The instant he backed off she flung open the door and hurried to the elevator.

By the time she reached the street the panic had gripped her in its vicious talons. The pain in her skull all but blinded her.

She understood beyond a shadow of a doubt, that he knew.

He knew she was lying.

CHAPTER FIVE

Elizabeth had little choice but to work long hours today and tomorrow, even if it was the weekend. She'd fallen seriously behind on her schedule with the funeral and the interrogations related to Ned's murder. Not to mention the worry and guilt slowing her usual pace. She would never survive as a criminal. She just wasn't cut out for a life of deception.

The thought brought Agent MacBride to mind. She hoped she never heard from him again. A little shiver chased over her flesh, reminding her that she might not have heard from him, but she'd noticed someone watching her. As she'd gone home last night and the moment she had pulled out onto the street this morning a dark sedan slid in behind her. Even Boomer had noticed the feds hanging around.

MacBride had warned her he'd be watching.

But what if it wasn't him or his men? What if it was whoever murdered Ned? The thought had an icy chill sinking deeper into her bones. *Just stop.*

Borrowing trouble wasn't going to do her any good. She'd worried enough for several lifetimes during the past two weeks. Besides, Boomer was certain her tail was *fibbies*, as he called them. He swore he could spot a federal agent from a mile away—they all looked the same. Same fancy suits, same designer sunglasses, and the same superior attitude.

Boomer was right about the attitude, she decided as she put the lid back on the fresh bucket of paint she'd had to open an hour or so ago. MacBride had enough cocky male attitude for a dozen men. That much testosterone in one guy could be unnerving. She shivered. Only this time it had nothing to do with fear and everything to do with awareness.

Okay. Time to call it a day. Whenever she started fantasizing about the guy attempting to pin a murder rap on her, it was definitely time for a break. It was late. She was tired and she had no choice but to work tomorrow. Working on Sunday was her least favorite thing to do, but finishing up this loft was essential. She'd just have to grin and bear it come morning. She glanced at the time on her cell. It was well past ten p.m. and she'd obviously gotten punchy. Too little sleep and far too much pressure, not a good combination under any circumstances. A decent night's sleep would do wonders for her ability to think straight. The final finishing touches could wait until morning. But she wouldn't ask Boomer to help on Sunday. It was bad enough she'd called him in today. He probably still had a social life.

"I'll finish up here," she said to Boomer when he noticed her putting away her tools. "You go on. I'll see you on Monday."

A frown creased his brow. "I'll just hang around and walk you out," he offered, ever the protector.

She shook her head. He'd already put in far more hours than his meager salary covered. "No. Really. I'll be okay." She shrugged. "Who's going to bother me with my very own federal agent watching?"

He crossed to the opposite side of the room and peered out the window. "He's still out there, all right." Boomer muttered a couple of inventive curses. "I don't know why you put up with it. They got no right watching you like this."

"It's okay." She ushered him into the dimly lit hallway and pointed to the elevator. "Now go. I'll be fine."

Reluctance slowing his step, Boomer shuffled to the only exit. He hesitated before boarding the antique lift. "Don't let 'em see you sweat, Elizabeth." His gaze settled on hers. "We both know you didn't kill that prick." He pushed open the iron bars that served as a door to the elevator, then paused to look back at her once more before boarding. "But he deserved exactly what he got."

Boomer stepped into the elevator and pulled the bars closed before setting it into motion. His gaze remained steady on hers until he was out of sight. A new worry nagged at her as she shuffled back into the loft.

How often had she complained about Ned in front of Boomer? She hadn't told him everything, but she'd gone on and on about how he'd used her, how he'd hurt her.

Surely Boomer hadn't—

No! She refused to believe any such thing. MacBride's innuendo about Boomer's past was messing with her head. She knew Boomer. He wouldn't kill another human being any more than she would.

Elizabeth made quick work of putting away the tools of her trade. She refused to dwell on a concept as ridiculous as one involving Boomer and murder. The whole idea was just another indicator of how badly she needed a good night's sleep.

When she was ready to go, she glanced out the window to see if the sedan was still there. Yep. Right there in the alley across the street. The driver had backed in so he could pull out behind her without any real effort. She wondered if cops and agents were trained to do that to ensure they didn't lose their surveillance target while turning around. Probably.

As the old lift lowered to the still-under-construction area that would eventually serve as a sophisticated lobby for the building, she couldn't help thinking what a monumental waste of time the surveillance of her movements really was. If the feds expended half as much effort on finding the real murderer as they did on watching her, they might have solved the case by now.

By the time she exited the building, she'd worked up a pretty good head of steam. Instead of climbing into her old beat-up truck, she marched across the street and right up to the sedan parked in the alley.

She banged on the driver's window. "Why do you keep watching me?" Any good sense she'd possessed was now lost to exhaustion and fury.

For a few seconds she wasn't sure whoever was on the other side of the tinted glass intended to respond, then the door opened. She fell back a couple of steps. What if Boomer had been wrong? What if this wasn't one of MacBride's pals?

Agent MacBride himself emerged from the vehicle. He towered over her with only the car door between them. The usual elegant suit jacket was missing. A white shirt, weary from a long day's wear, stretched over his broad shoulders. The top two buttons were open and the navy tie hung loose at his throat. His short hair looked as if he'd run his hands through it repeatedly, leaving it tousled in a manner that could only be called sexy.

Inwardly, she groaned. Why would she notice that? What in the world was wrong with her? She was losing her mind. That was the only reasonable explanation.

"I told you I'd be watching, Elizabeth."

Damn her treacherous emotions. The very sound of his voice sent a quake through her. She wrapped her arms around herself and glared up at him, determined not to allow him to see another indication of weakness. "This is ridiculous. Why aren't you chasing the real bad guys, instead of harassing me?"

He eased around the door and shoved it shut behind him, putting his body mere inches from hers. "We both know why I'm watching you, don't we?"

Anger flamed inside her. "Did you call my attorney?" She definitely had, as much as she'd hated to—the retainer alone had set her back two months' rent, but her landlady had been understanding and offered to allow her to pay the rent a little late. Thank God there were still a few compassionate people left in this world.

"Do I need to call your attorney?" he countered smoothly. "I thought maybe we could settle this between us."

Her breath stilled in her lungs as that fierce gaze came to rest on her lips. What was he doing? Was this a new strategy? Had he noticed her physical attraction to him and decided to play on it? Was he that desperate to pin this on her? Or maybe he actually thought she was guilty.

"I'm tired, MacBride," she admitted, too exhausted to fight this battle now. "Just leave me alone, okay? I don't need this crap."

She gave him her back and headed toward her truck on the other side of the street. Damn him. She was sick to death of being accused. What was it about her that made people believe she could commit a crime so heinous? Even the sheriff back home, a man who had known her since the day she was born, had initially believed her sorry-ass brother-in-law over her. But, with her father's desperate prodding, he'd dug more deeply, finally discovering the truth. She was innocent. Just like now. Only that time she actually had stabbed her no good brother-in-law. It was either that or let him beat her pregnant sister to death. Unfortunately, the bastard had survived to torment Elizabeth and her sister a while longer.

Who knew? Maybe it was a guy thing. Maybe they had to side with each other, protect the brotherhood at all costs. If there was a woman anywhere nearby to blame, that was the preferred route.

"Did he help you do it? Will he go to jail for you?"

MacBride's voice stopped her dead in her tracks midway across the street. She turned slowly, afraid to ask what he meant by that statement and equally afraid not to demand an answer.

"What the hell are you talking about?"

"Your assistant, Boomer. Did he talk you into it? Maybe the two of you have something going on and he got jealous of your relationship with the good doctor. Younger guys are like that, you know. Is he the one who tied up Harrison?"

No matter that she was exhausted, white-hot fury exploded inside her. She clenched her hands into fists and shook with the effort to restrain the outrage when she spoke. "This isn't going to work, MacBride." She scarcely recognized the voice as her own. "I didn't kill him and Boomer didn't either. If you have some kind of evidence that leads you to believe I'm guilty, then arrest me. If not, leave me and my assistant alone."

She spun away and started forward again. This just kept getting worse and worse. He was like a dog with a bone. He just wouldn't let it go. All she had to do was reach her truck, climb in, and she was out of there. She would not waste another moment of her time on this man or his silly suppositions.

"But you can't prove you actually went home after being stood up at the restaurant."

The words were spoken softly, yet there was no denying the determination in his tone. He wasn't going to stop scratching around until he uncovered everything.

She hesitated once more and summoned the necessary courage to face him yet again. "That's right." She looked straight at him. Between the streetlights and the moon, she could see all she needed to—more than she wanted to. "I don't have anyone to vouch for my whereabouts. I can't prove anything. You'll just have to take my word for it."

Enough already. If he had evidence he would arrest her. But this intimidation had to stop. She'd had all she could take.

"I can do that."

Startled, she wasn't sure what to say for a second or two. "You believe me?"

He laughed, a low, sensual sound that made her want to scream at herself for being such a fool. Why was she always, always attracted to the wrong kind of man?

"You said I'd have to take your word for it. I can do that if," he paused, "you're willing to repeat those words during a polygraph."

Fear paralyzed her. She couldn't take a polygraph. He would have proof of her lies then.

"Why the hesitation?" He shrugged. "If you're telling the truth you have nothing to lose and everything to gain."

"I thought polygraphs weren't admissible in court," she retaliated. Her heart thundered. This was it. She was done. He had her. He would never in a million years believe her story now. She'd lied. He knew it. She was doomed.

"You say you're telling the truth. I'm simply offering you an opportunity to prove that assertion."

"I'll...I'll have to speak to my attorney."

He moved closer, one deliberate step at a time until he was back in her personal space. She couldn't have moved had her life depended on it. The fear had nailed her to the spot. She couldn't move. Couldn't think what to do or say next.

"All I want from you, Elizabeth, is the truth. If you're really innocent, as you say you are, then you must know your uncooperative actions are slowing down this case. You're essentially helping a murderer to continue walking the streets. If you want to clear your name and get this investigation pointed in the right direction, then help me."

"I...can't help you. I don't know anything."

Mac stared down into those frightened amber eyes and it was all he could do not to reach out to her, not to comfort her. She was scared to death, and every instinct urged him to reach out. The feelings were totally unacceptable. He gritted his teeth and got himself back under control. She was a suspect, the primary suspect in his opinion, in a murder investigation. He needed her cooperation. Losing his focus was not an option.

"Did you have sex with Harrison that night? Did you go to his place looking for him when he didn't show up at the restaurant? Did you have a fight? Maybe you didn't mean to kill him. Maybe it was a game that got out of hand. I know about the kinky sex he enjoyed, and the games he played."

She shook her head, her whole body primed with the urge to flee. He recognized the posture. But something, the fear maybe, held her firmly in place.

"I didn't—"

"Don't lie to me, Elizabeth," he pressed. "You've already lied to me once." He'd known from the moment he first laid eyes on her that she was hiding something.

She blinked. "Why would I lie to you? I didn't kill him."

He tried to read the other emotion cluttering her face. "Is it the video? Are you afraid your relationship with Harrison will be exposed? Is that why you're holding back?"

She shook her head again. "He…he used me. It was a mistake." She looked away then. "I made a mistake." Her gaze flew back to his. "But I didn't kill him.

"Are you the one who scratched him when you argued?" Mac went on. "Is it your pubic hair we found on his body?"

The bravado vanished in an instant "I told you I went home after leaving the restaurant."

"Why don't I believe that?" His gut told him she was telling the truth about her innocence where the murder was concerned, but there was something more. She was lying about something and he had to know what it was. He felt confident the NYPD would eventually solve the homicide, but he wanted anything she might know that would help him find the evidence needed to solve his case. If keeping her terrified was the only way to make that happen, then so be it.

She held up her hands, palms out. "Enough." She backed away a step. "You can arrest me or you can let me go home. Which will it be?"

His cell vibrated. "Go home," he told her as he reached for the interruption. "But remember, I'll be watching."

Without responding to his blatant threat she stormed away. He let go a disgusted breath and took the call. "MacBride."

"Brannigan just called," Duncan explained. "Another of Harrison's patients is dead. I'm on my way there now."

"Where?" Mac double-timed it back to his car.

"Mercer Street. Willidean Delinsky." Duncan provided the exact address. "She goes by the name Deana Adele. She's that supermodel who got busted for drugs early last year. You know the one who does the Sass ads."

Sass was a designer perfume that was all the rage with younger women. Mac definitely remembered the model. Blond, glamorous. She'd been at Harrison's funeral wearing a red dress that turned every head in the place. "What's the connection?" He knew there was one, otherwise Brannigan would never in a millions years have called them in on his turf. At least the guy was making an effort to cooperate now.

"Same MO as the last one. Panties shoved in her mouth and her throat was slit."

Mac swore. "I'll meet you there."

The scene was every bit as gruesome as the one involving Vanessa Bumbalough. The MO appeared to be near identical. Only this time Mac got to see the victim before her body was removed. She'd been tied to her elegant bed, sexually assaulted and then murdered in the same manner. The spray of blood adorning the bed and the covers testified to the violence. There was far less splatter on the wall this time. The unsub had apparently learned his lesson and opted to slit his victim's throat after she was tied to the bed. Or maybe he'd wanted to watch her face—to see her die—as the blood pumped from her body.

As Mac stood back and viewed the undisturbed crime scene, his predominant thought was that this was an execution. Someone had demoralized and executed this woman. This was no random act of sexual violence. This murder had purpose and calculation. Again, the rest of the home was undisturbed. Not a single item looked out of place. No sign of forced entry. This building didn't have a doorman but whoever had entered the premises had been allowed to do so by a resident who pressed a button and disengaged the lock barring the entrance. It was the only way inside. Brannigan already had officers canvassing the residents to see if anyone had buzzed in a visitor in the past twenty-four hours.

The ME had put the time of death at six to eight hours ago. They wouldn't have more concrete details until after the autopsy. The victim's live-in boyfriend had come home late from the office and discovered the body. Brannigan was still grilling him in the next room. But Mac didn't need to hear any of the interrogation. This had nothing to do with the boyfriend.

This was about Ned Harrison.

Mac was sure of it He'd felt that nudge at the Bumbalough crime scene, but now it was more than a mere nudge. Someone had murdered Ned Harrison and now appeared bent on killing his patients. But why? What did Vanessa Bumbalough and Deana Adele have to do with anything? Why these two patients? What did they have in common besides Harrison and how did any of their murders connect to the Gentlemen's Association?

Those were the answers he needed.

The possibility that these two women would not be the last abruptly surfaced in the flood of scenarios crashing into his consciousness.

Elizabeth.

She had been Harrison's patient and lover, and she had attended his funeral.

A cold hard fist of fear jammed into Mac's gut. She might very well be hiding the answer to all this and not know it. He thought of the video of Elizabeth Young and then the ones of the two dead women. Was it simply being a patient of Harrison's that marked these women for death, or was it the videos? Each one had likely already been viewed by the Gentlemen's Association, whose membership was spread across the country like a disease building toward an epidemic. It could be any one of those sick bastards. If someone high enough in the association had realized that Harrison was under federal surveillance, his death may have been ordered.

But why the women? To throw the investigation off track? To point toward a serial killer?

There had to be something more.

And somehow Elizabeth Young was involved. He was certain of it. Whether or not she was guilty of murder, she most likely needed protection.

He motioned for Duncan to step into the hallway with him.

Once out of earshot of the crime scene techs and any of Brannigan's men, he said quietly, "I want you to go straight to Elizabeth Young's apartment and stay there until I relieve you."

Duncan frowned. "But what about—"

"Go now." Urgency had tied his gut in knots. He didn't want her alone. "I'll be there as soon as I can."

None too pleased to have to give up a crime scene for a simple stakeout, Duncan nodded and headed out without further argument He had a lot to learn, but he never failed to follow orders.

Relaxing a fraction, Mac returned to the master bedroom where the ME was preparing to remove Deana Adele's body. The ordeal to come would serve as further violation and injustice to her physical remains, but, hopefully, it would help identify her murderer.

She and Vanessa Bumbalough were the only witnesses they had so far and both were dead.

Elizabeth climbed out of the tub, quickly dried off, and pulled on her robe. She felt better already. She'd needed that long, steamy soak. Deciding a cup of hot cocoa was in order, she padded into the kitchen. As she poured the milk into the pan to warm, she attempted to block all thoughts of Agent MacBride.

She failed miserably.

If he forced the issue, she would have no choice but to tell him the truth or take the test. It was too late to call her attorney, but she knew if she refused the test, it would be taken as a sign of guilt.

She was damned if she did and damned if she didn't.

When she thought about the way MacBride had looked at her lips, heat swirled inside her. Her fingers instinctively went there, tracing her mouth, her mind struggling with the question of why he would have looked at her that way. As if he wanted to kiss her, as if he was attracted to her. But that was impossible. He only wanted one thing.

To solve his case at her expense.

All this surveillance was nothing but intimidation. Her attorney had confirmed her suspicions, but she hadn't really needed him to. She'd already been down this road.

It was these other feelings that worried her. She hadn't been attracted to a man sexually since Brian. Sure she'd had an affair with Ned, but that had been about pure physical release and nothing more. She'd needed someone in that way to prove it hadn't been her fault that Brian dumped her. Ned had known it and he'd taken advantage of her vulnerability.

This was different. This was overwhelming. Maybe it was nothing but a combination of all the events that had befallen her in the past year. The stress was making her crazy. She was so damned tired. Agent MacBride was strong and had that take-charge mentality down to a science. He made her want to trust him...to lean on him.

She poured her warm milk into a cup and slowly stirred in the cocoa and sugar. All this time she'd been telling herself she could make it on her own. That she didn't need anyone to support her.

Dammit, she didn't. If she hadn't gotten behind on her schedule with all this insanity surrounding Ned's murder, she would be great, financially and otherwise.

She did not need anyone taking care of her. She was strong and self-reliant. She always had been. *Deep breath.* This too would pass. That was her mantra of late. She sipped her cocoa and wandered into the living room. It wasn't as if it was the first time she'd been faced with seemingly insurmountable obstacles to overcome.

Feeling a little more relaxed, she set her cocoa on the table next to the sofa and clicked on the television. She might as well catch the news before she hit the sack. Although it was late April and the weather was good for this time of year, a sudden winter storm wasn't unheard of. When self-employed, you had to stay on top of anything that might set back the work schedule.

Before she could sit down, her telephone rang. The caller ID display read *blocked call.* She answered on the second ring. "Hello." A beat of silence, then the distinctive click of the party at the other end of the line hanging up.

"Jerk," she muttered. She hated telemarketers. Why the hell would they call so late?

She was so caught up in her frustration with the caller that a knock on the door made her jump.

Renewed anger fired through her. If MacBride was knocking on her door in the middle of the night, Mrs. Polk would not be happy. The elderly woman didn't want anyone living above her who partied or had late-night guests. Elizabeth couldn't blame her. She was an elderly woman who supplemented her income by renting out her unused upstairs. She didn't need any additional turmoil in her life. Who did?

Too furious to think rationally, Elizabeth rushed to the door in her bare feet before a second knock rattled the hinges, unlocked and jerked it open.

The tiny landing atop the private rear stairs stood empty. She stared out over the narrow alleyway that separated Mrs. Polk's small frame house from her neighbor's. The moonlight that managed to penetrate the darkness and surrounding trees provided little in the way of illumination. Elizabeth blinked and looked again. *Nothing.* She stepped out onto the landing and squinted into the darkness to survey the steep set of stairs leading to the drive where her truck was parked. Nothing appeared out of place.

Had she imagined the knock? There'd been only one. Maybe a passing car backfired or someone walking by on the street made the sound. If someone had knocked, he'd moved mighty fast down those steps to disappear into the darkness before she opened the door. She heaved a sigh, evidently she was more exhausted than she'd realized. After closing and locking the door, she had another thought. What if her relentless federal agent had called and then thrown something at her door just to make sure she was home? Maybe MacBride was worried she would skip town.

Indignation burst inside her. She strode to the front window and stared down at the street. A dark sedan sat at the curb directly across the expanse of pavement from the house.

"Bastard." A smile slid across her face. She let the curtain fall back into place and rushed to find her purse. Dumping the contents, she rifled through the mess until she found MacBride's card. She'd punched in the number and heard the first ring before she allowed the second thoughts to surface. When she would have hung up, he answered.

"MacBride."

Renewed fury flared inside her. "Look, you pompous jerk, I don't appreciate being harassed in the middle of the night."

"Elizabeth?"

"Don't pretend you don't know what I'm talking about," she went on. "I can't stop you from watching my house or my job site, but I will not tolerate you calling and hanging up, or knocking on my door and then disappearing. Just leave me alone!"

She ended the call and shut off her phone. MacBride was not going to bother her again tonight.

CHAPTER SIX

Before Mac could ask what the hell Elizabeth was talking about, she ended the call. He replayed her words. Someone had apparently called her and hung up, and then knocked on her door and disappeared.

Why the hell would Duncan do anything as ridiculous as that? If he'd wanted to ensure the suspect was indeed at home, Duncan should have asked when he called, not hung up.

Something dark and foreboding crawled up Mac's spine. He put through a call to Duncan's cell and held his breath until his partner answered.

"Duncan."

The noise in the background made Mac frown. Horns blowing. People arguing. "Duncan, what the hell's going on? Elizabeth Young—"

"I was just about to call you," Duncan shouted into the phone. "I've been in a little fender bender. I'm trying to talk the investigating officer into releasing me now."

He wasn't even at Elizabeth's house.

Mac's blood ran cold. Then who the hell knocked on her door?

He was on the road before the potential answers—all bad—formed in his brain.

Despite driving like a bat out of hell and zooming through the Lincoln Tunnel, which would have been impossible had it not been the middle of the night, it still took Mac far longer to reach Leonia and Elizabeth's apartment than he would have liked. He tried calling her back, but all he got was her voicemail.

When he finally reached her address, he didn't bother to covertly park on the street. He roared straight into the driveway and skidded to a halt right behind her beat-up old truck. He was out of his car before it stopped rocking and took the exterior stairs to her door two at a time. Despite his hurry, he took note of each vehicle parked near the house on either side of the street. The surrounding homes were quiet and dark. Mac knew this section of the small town. Low crime rate, mostly blue-collar workers, all probably tucked in for the night in anticipation of church on Sunday morning.

Sucking in a deep breath to calm the thrashing in his chest, he pounded heavily on her door. He refused to consider that he might be too late already or that he was overreacting. He shook his head as he let go a ragged breath of fatigue. He shouldn't have left her without surveillance. Every instinct had warned him that she was somehow relevant to his investigation. For days now he or one of his men had watched her every move.

And what had he done tonight? He'd left her on her own.

The door opened just as he raised his fist to pound on it again. Relief, mixed with a kind of vague defeat, gushed through him at the sight of her.

Her hair mussed and her glasses askew, she stared at him for a moment before recognition flared. In the next beat her eyes widened in surprise that was quickly followed by unbridled fury.

"What are you trying to do? Wake the whole neighborhood?"

Highly trained agent that he was, he couldn't even respond when faced with the fact that she stood in the doorway wearing a t-shirt that scarcely reached the tops of her thighs. Backlit by an interior light, the gentle curves of her slender figure were clearly silhouetted beneath the thin, white cotton fabric.

Before he could stop himself, he gazed down the length of her, all the way to her neatly manicured toes. But it was the return trip that did the most damage to his control. Long toned legs, a slim torso and small breasts that jutted firmly against the flimsy fabric covering them, and on to a slender throat that curved upward into delicate cheeks and full lips. When his gaze at last came back to rest on hers, the look of rage in those amber eyes jerked him from the trance of lust he'd lapsed into.

"I'm calling the police." With those snapped words, she executed an about-face and left him standing there like the unwelcome guest he was.

His own temper flaring, Mac crossed the threshold uninvited and slammed the door behind him. "And tell them what?"

The frightened rabbit expression that captured her pretty face sent him hurtling back into reality. What the hell was wrong with him? He never lost it like this. It was that damned video. He'd watched more than two dozens but it was hers that haunted him. Made him ache to see more. Fool he was, he couldn't not want her.

Elizabeth couldn't believe her eyes, much less her ears. Maybe it was her, but she didn't think so. MacBride was behaving strangely, and she didn't know whether to run for her life or slap some sense into him. Either way she was reasonably sure he had no intention of backing off.

"What is it you want, Agent MacBride?" She planted her hands on her waist and marched straight up to him, lifting her chin defiantly. How dare he barge into her home in the middle of the night! It was bad enough she'd endured his shenanigans with the phone call and the anonymous knock on the door. "I'm sick and tired of you and your people following me around." When she was toe-to-toe with him, she poked him in the chest with her forefinger. He flinched. That mere touch sent an electrical charge surging through her, but she quickly recovered. "This is blatant harassment."

"You called me, remember?"

The sound of his voice shimmered over her already exposed nerve endings. "Only because you called first and hung up like a kid playing a prank." She huffed a sigh of exasperation. "And let's not forget you knocked on my door and then vanished like Houdini. What'd you think? That I'd sneaked out the back door to go murder someone else? I don't even have a back door." Control snapped. "Why are you doing this?"

As she fought to regain her composure, something changed in his eyes, and that lean, chiseled profile softened just the tiniest bit. "That's just it," he said. Even his voice was softer now. "I didn't call you and I damn sure didn't knock on your door until just a few seconds ago."

Mac watched the confusion claim her, lining her smooth brow, parting those luscious lips. "One of your men then," she refuted. "I opened the door," she gestured to the one he'd slammed only moments before, "and no one was there." Her gaze flew to his. "You said you'd be watching. I saw the car."

"I didn't follow you home tonight. No one on my team followed you. Can you describe the vehicle you saw?"

She shook her head in answer to his question, as well as in denial of the possibility that obviously scared the hell out of her. Someone had been watching her, all right. "I...I don't understand."

Mac squeezed his hands into fists and resisted the urge to reach for her. Every moment with her was a battle for one kind of control or the other. "Is there anyone in your neighborhood who would do this sort of thing as a joke?" he asked, determined to keep this discussion on track. "A friend or neighborhood kid who gets off on scaring others, maybe?"

Her head moved jerkily from side to side. "All the neighbors are older, like Mrs. Polk." She laughed, but the sound held no humor. "No way could one of them have knocked and gotten down the stairs and out of sight before I opened the door." She seemed to wilt beneath the weight of the realization that she'd just dismissed the safest, most reasonable possibilities, leaving only one alternative.

Mac crossed to the door, opened it and moved out onto the small landing to survey the situation from her vantage point He peered over the side and concluded that even jumping over the railing wouldn't have been a big deal for a younger person, an athletic type. He knew he could do it easily. But if her neighbors were around Mrs. Polk's age, seventy or so, there was no way one of them could have taken that leap and rushed away. He glanced up and down the narrow alley that separated the house from its neighbor. With the numerous overgrown shrubs and small, detached garages, there were plenty of places to hide. For that matter, a quick jump over the rail and simply darting back under the stairs would be sufficient camouflage from here.

He stepped back inside and closed the door. During his short absence Elizabeth had donned a tattered robe. With her arms wrapped around herself, she looked incredibly vulnerable and very much like a frightened little girl in need of a hug.

But she was no little girl. Those full lips were parted slightly as if she was on the verge of asking something but feared the answer. She'd straightened her glasses and thrust her fingers through her hair, leaving the silky mass hanging loosely around her slender shoulders.

Beating himself up for noticing every little thing about her would accomplish nothing, but somehow he had to get a grip here. Right now was the perfect time to push for answers. She was vulnerable. Yet, it took every ounce of determination he possessed to do the job. "It's time to stop playing games, Elizabeth. Tell me what it is you're hiding and we'll get this mystery solved." He stared directly into her eyes. "You won't be safe until this thing is settled. I know it and I think deep down you know do as well."

The delicate line of her jaw hardened a fraction. "Are you admitting that you believe me when I say I didn't have anything to do with Ned's," she blinked rapidly, "with Dr. Harrison's murder?"

He wanted to believe she was capable of a slick move like this—that the whole phone-call-knock-on-the-door thing was a hoax designed to garner sympathy—but he knew better. No way could she fake that kind of fear. He'd seen it in her eyes when she realized it hadn't been the authorities outside her door or on the other end of that call. She'd been truly frightened.

Still, on the off chance that he was a bigger fool than he already suspected… "No," he told her flatly. "I'm admitting that I believe someone else knows your secret and maybe that secret is putting you in the same kind of danger Harrison found himself in."

Direct hit. Her breath caught and the stark fear glittered in her eyes once more. Now all he had to do was move in for the kill.

Stepping closer—into her personal space, a move he already knew unsettled her—he pressed, "Tell me the truth, Elizabeth. I can't help you if you don't." She tried backing away from him, but he just kept advancing until she backed into the sofa. "Do you know where I was when you called tonight?"

She couldn't breathe, couldn't think, couldn't escape those penetrating blue eyes. *Please,* she wanted to cry, *just leave me alone. I didn't do this awful thing!* But she couldn't speak. She could only stare into those accusing eyes and pray he wouldn't see the truth in her own.

"I was at the scene of a ten fifty-four. Do you know what a ten fifty-four is, Elizabeth?"

He was closer, yet she wasn't sure he'd moved. But something about his savage demeanor made her feel as if he was right on top of her, waiting for her to break.

"A dead body," he said in answer to his own question. "There's been another homicide."

Emotion quaked through her. Another murder. God, she didn't want to know this. Why didn't he just leave? It couldn't have anything to do with her. She blinked back the sheen of tears that threatened to wreck the remnants of her already shredded composure and stared back at him in defiance. "What does that have to do with me?"

"Did you know Deana Adele, the model?" he went on, ignoring her question, his face mere inches from hers. "She was one of Dr. Harrison's patients, too. Maybe you saw her at the funeral."

The blond. Elizabeth knew instantly. In the red dress. A model. Living large and fast. She remembered her. She'd read about her and her trouble with drugs, last year maybe. At the time, she'd wondered if the model had been covering up for someone else, too. But at the funeral Elizabeth hadn't gotten a good look at her face. Hadn't recalled who she was then.

And now it no longer mattered.

She was dead

Homicide.

That meant murder.

Dear God.

Her stomach rolled over.

"Two of Harrison's patients have been murdered since his funeral," he said pointedly. "Don't you find that strangely ironic?"

The room tilted and then started to spin. Nausea boiled up in her throat. Elizabeth was going to be sick.

Mac moved back a step as Elizabeth pushed away from him and ran from the room. Restraining the need to go after her, he took a moment to calm the crazy mixture of emotions raging inside him. Then he followed. He couldn't take any chances that she might make a run for it. In four steps he'd crossed the room and entered the small hall. As he reached the closed bathroom door, his concerns were allayed by the sound of her violent retching.

Guilt stabbed him right in the gut as he leaned against the wall next to the door. He'd pushed her to the edge. Damn. Sympathy wasn't supposed to enter into this. Where was his usual detachment? Why the hell couldn't he maintain proper distance?

He released a weary breath and refused to consider the answer to either of those questions.

Eventually he heard the toilet flush and the water running in the basin, then a minute or so later she opened the door. "I'd like you to leave now," she announced with a good deal more strength than she looked capable of managing.

"I need some answers first."

She ripped off her glasses and rubbed her eyes, then glared at him. "Don't you ever give up? I'm telling you I don't know anything!"

He stepped nearer to her. Didn't miss the flicker of uncertainty in her eyes. "Yes, you do. I'll keep coming back until you tell me everything."

She pushed her glasses back into place and shoved her hair from her face with unsteady hands. "You're wasting your time, Agent MacBride."

Another thought poked its way through the jumble of theories attempting to coalesce in his brain. "How did your ex-fiancé take your affair with Dr. Harrison?"

Elizabeth blinked, taken aback by the question. What was he fishing for now? Didn't the man get it? She didn't know anything relevant to his case. "Brian and I broke up months ago."

MacBride shrugged, the move casual, but his expression was anything but casual. "That may be, but he had to be pissed off when he learned he'd been replaced by a hotshot shrink. Wasn't Harrison a friend of his?"

A frown worried her lips. She'd seen Ned at some of the parties she and Brian had attended. She'd even seen Brian talk to Ned from time to time, but then, he talked to everyone. Not once in their nine-month relationship had she heard Brian mention Ned. Ned certainly never mentioned Brian other than in the context of how her breakup with him added to the stress that brought on her panic attacks.

"I don't...think so," she admitted in all honesty. "I suppose you could call them casual acquaintances."

MacBride was watching her so closely that she could almost feel his eyes on her. She tugged the lapels of her robe tighter around her, but it wasn't her body that held his attention. He was studying her face, analyzing her responses, looking for signs of deception.

"It's late," she said, squaring her shoulders and moving slightly away. "I'd like you to go now."

For one long moment she was sure he intended to argue the point, but to her surprise, he didn't.

"I'll be outside all night," he said, instead. "When I go, one of my men will take over."

She nodded, too grateful now for a bodyguard of sorts to be angry.

With one final, lingering look, he turned and made his way back into her living room. She followed, abruptly and painfully conscious of her meager furnishings and less-than-spectacular housekeeping skills. She wasn't exactly a slob, but she wasn't neat, either.

At the door he hesitated. "This door doesn't have a peephole or a dead bolt. Think about getting both installed. In the meantime, at least ask who's there before you open the door."

Oddly, she sensed his words were well meant. That he cared what happened to her.

Yeah, right.

He only wanted to keep his prime suspect alive and well until he could nail her for murder and close the case.

"Thanks for the advice." She failed miserably at sounding appreciative.

His gaze bored into hers. "I'm serious, Elizabeth. I don't want you to end up dead."

With that profound statement he left.

For several seconds after the door closed, she could only stand there absorbing the impact and ramifications of his words.

Two of Ned's patients had been murdered in the past few days. Coincidence? Apparently the FBI didn't think so.

Cold, bony fingers of fear clutched at her. Maybe MacBride was right. Maybe her life was in danger. She locked the door, wishing she had a deadbolt. She hurried over to the front window and drew back the curtain. Just as he promised, MacBride backed out onto the street and parked directly in front of the house. Relief flooded her.

Vanessa Bumbalough was dead. Deana Adele was dead.

Who would be next?

Elizabeth half stumbled to the sofa in her haste and snatched up the phone. She turned it on and called Gloria. Pacing the floor as she waited for her friend to answer, she prayed. *Please, God, let her be home. And safe.*

When a groggy hello came, Elizabeth blurted, "We have to talk!"

Mac waited patiently for Duncan to answer his cell phone. When Mac had headed to Elizabeth's apartment, he'd ordered his partner to the Deana Adele crime scene. "They find anything else?" he asked without preamble.

"Nothing. The techs found dozens of different prints. The lady apparently had a lot of guests. Since she and the Bumbalough woman ran in the same circles, there's no telling how many sets matching the previous scene they'll find."

A lot of nothing leading nowhere. Mac rubbed his eyes and stared up at the light in the window of Elizabeth's apartment. He had a bad feeling about this. A very bad feeling.

"I'll maintain surveillance on Elizabeth Young tonight," he informed his partner. "I'll need you here to relieve me by eight in the morning. Tonight, I want you to track down a Brian Novak of Design Horizons and have him meet me at my office at nine sharp."

Duncan snorted. "Tomorrow's Sunday, Mac. How can I—?"

"I don't care if it's Christmas," Mac shot back. "Have the guy at my office at nine sharp."

"Will do," Duncan replied sheepishly. "Anything else?"

Mac exhaled a weary breath. "That's it. Call me if there's any news from the ME."

He ended the call and dropped the phone on the console. It was going to be a long night. Shifting until he found a comfortable spot, he considered the layout around Elizabeth's apartment. She had no security, and the surrounding area was an intruder's wet dream. Everyone went to bed early and likely didn't hear as well as they used to. If someone wanted her, getting to her would be easy. She worked long hours and probably slept like a rock during the few hours of rest she got.

If she was the innocent she insisted she was and the latest turn in this case evolved into what he suspected, she could very well be in grave danger.

Whether she was a suspect, a material witness, or simply a woman in jeopardy because she got mixed up with the wrong guy, Mac was duty bound to protect her.

Problem was, duty had nothing to do with his incessant need to stick close to her. He was plunging headfirst into personal involvement with a suspect. Something he never permitted.

But there didn't appear to be a damned thing he could do about it this time. Some part of him was hell-bent on saving the woman, whether she wanted to be saved or not.

SUNDAY, APRIL 26

Elizabeth slept maybe two hours the entire night. Before sunrise she was pacing the floor. At six she'd forced herself to bake her Sunday favorite, blueberry muffins. And she'd made a strong pot of coffee. The way she felt at the moment it would take the entire pot to get her through the day. But she had to work. She simply had no choice.

She pulled on her jeans and a t-shirt, rolled on a clean pair of socks and then slipped on her sneakers. Another cup of coffee and she'd be good to go.

She stilled, her gaze drawn to the front window. How was MacBride faring? She moved to the window and peeked around the edge of the curtain. He was still there. The driver's-side window had been lowered to let in the cool morning air. As she watched, he scrubbed a hand over his face. She could just imagine how he felt. Exhausted. Hungry.

"Dammit."

No matter how many times she told herself that her most recent problems were entirely his fault, she just couldn't help feeling bad about him sitting out there in a cold car after having no sleep.

Admitting defeat, she filled a thermal to-go cup with coffee and wrapped a couple of muffins in a paper towel. The least she could do was feed him. He had, after all, spent the night watching over her. The thought had her experiencing more of that awareness she could no longer deny. She was sexually attracted to the man.

She groaned. What an idiot she was. Outright asking for trouble. Ignoring the alarm bells jangling in her head, she pulled on a jacket and marched out the door, down the steps and across the street. He caught sight of her before her sneakers hit the pavement and he was climbing out of the car.

"Is everything all right?" Those blue eyes surveyed her from head to toe.

Just like last night, she could feel his eyes roaming her body. And damned if he didn't look even better with a night's growth of beard shadowing that chiseled jaw. "Everything's just peachy," she lied, forcing the forbidden thoughts to the farthest recesses of her mind. "I thought you might be hungry."

Actually he looked ravenous. But then, she hadn't noticed that look in his eyes until after he'd given her the onceover. She scolded herself for allowing such a silly notion. Rich guys like MacBride didn't bother with working girls like her. Well, working girls in the sense of blue-collar types. She'd been born into a blue-collar family and she was damned proud of it. Her short stint in the high-end design world hadn't gone so well. She didn't belong there.

"Thanks." He reached for the cup. "I was having fantasies about coffee."

She blinked away the fantasies she'd been having that had nothing to do with coffee. "It's black. I didn't know if you liked cream or sugar."

"Black is perfect." He had a taste and moaned. "That hit the spot."

The sound of his satisfaction had her smiling and feeling entirely too warm. "Muffins." She thrust the still-warm baked goods at him and chastised herself again for being a total schmuck.

He set the coffee on the roof of his car and reached for the muffins.

His fingers brushed hers and butterflies took flight in her belly. She needed to go, *now*. "I have to get to the job site."

"On Sunday?"

Shoving her hands into her back pockets, she offered another of those careless shrugs. "Sometimes it's necessary." Unlike him, she had to really work for a living. Even then she didn't have money to throw around on extravagant clothes much less luxury cars. She stole a glance at the dark sedan he drove. Foreign, loaded, mega pricey. She'd bet those leather seats were heated, too. Must be nice. And here she'd felt sorry for him out here in his seventy-thousand-dollar car. How many ways could she prove herself a fool?

For a time they stood in silence. He consumed the muffins and coffee. Finally he tossed the napkin into his fancy car, then handed the cup back to her. "That hit the spot, thanks."

She accepted the cup, careful not to allow her fingers to graze his. She was already in enough trouble here. "It was the least I could do," she said before she thought. A flush heated her cheeks. "I mean… you did keep an eye on my place last night and I was pretty shaken up."

"You didn't think of anything you needed to tell me?"

Here they were again, right back at square one. "I told you—"

His cell phone buzzed, cutting off the rest of her words. He reached into his breast pocket and pulled out the slim device. "MacBride."

She looked away, not wanting to intrude. It could be his girlfriend. Or his wife. Before she could stop the move, she checked out his left hand for a ring.

No rings whatsoever.

She gave a little mental snort of self-disgust and forced her attention to the ground where it belonged. What an absolute idiot she was! He was the enemy. She was a pathetic woman who'd been dumped by her fiancé and taken advantage of by her shrink, to whom she'd paid top dollar to climb inside her head. He had, in turn, used what he'd learned to get inside her pants. Now, the FBI agent who wanted to charge her with the shrink's murder was somehow turning her on as well as inside out.

It just didn't get worse than this.

"Give me the address again." The steely tone drew Elizabeth's attention back to him. He listened intently, his face devoid of emotion. "I'm on my way."

She waited, her nerves jangling, as he put the phone away. His voice had sounded so ominous. Maybe there'd been a break in Ned's case. This whole nightmare couldn't be over soon enough for her.

He lifted his gaze to hers and said the last thing she wanted to hear. "There's been another murder. Cassandra Fowler."

Her heart took off at a gallop, the blood whooshing in her ears as it roared through her body. Even though she didn't recognize the name, he didn't have to say the rest. She already knew.

He glanced away briefly, then zoomed in on her with such ferocity that she almost drew back from the force of it. "Another of your former lover's patients."

Tension thickened between them. It felt different in a way she couldn't quite define.

"It's time to come clean, Elizabeth," he said grimly. "Before anyone else has to die."

CHAPTER SEVEN

The Lucky Strike bustled with activity at noon, even on Sunday. The cool downtown eatery was on Grand between Broadway and Wooster. Though incredibly hip, it wasn't the kind of place a girl had to worry about dressing up for. A good thing, too, since Elizabeth had come straight from her job site. She'd felt a panic attack coming on and had needed the long walk. Her private fed, the one named Duncan, had followed in his dark sedan, taking care to keep his distance. As soon as she'd arrived, the waitress had shown her to one of the wooden tables in the back and taken her drink order.

Despite all that had occurred the night before, as well as this morning, Elizabeth managed to complete the final details on the job. If she could get the second loft on the floor finished by the end of the upcoming week, she'd have it made. For a couple of months, anyway.

She fingered the mug of coffee and forced herself to focus on the events of the past week. As much as she didn't want to, she had to consider that something very sinister was happening and somehow it related to Ned and his dirty little secret. *Her* dirty little secret.

The bastard. Even in death he haunted her.

She repressed a shudder and once again wrapped her mind around the concept of serial murders. Whoever killed Ned could very well be the one killing his patients.

Maybe she should have ordered something far stronger than coffee. Feeling cold and alone, she glanced around the lively dining room with its French copper bar, seemingly carefree patrons, and attentive staff. Usually this place lifted her mood but today she couldn't shake the depressing feelings. People were dying.

There was always the off chance that the murders weren't even related.

"Yeah, right," she muttered. Maybe she could have gone along with that theory after the first woman was murdered. And maybe even the second. But the third…

Three women.

Three of Ned's patients.

In some instances the third time was considered the charm, but in this situation Elizabeth could only conceive that it was a sign. A sign of bad things to come.

She was a woman.

She had been one of Ned's patients.

If a list of future victims with those two common factors existed, her name would be on it.

How could this be happening? Surely the police would find and stop this killer. How many more women had to die before they figured out who this sick bastard was?

She moistened her lips, then clamped down on her lower one to stem the fear welling in her throat. What had those women done to deserve to die? Was their only mistake getting involved with Ned Harrison?

If her initial conclusion at the funeral was correct, then they had all likely slept with Ned, just as she had. But he was dead. He wasn't killing anyone. He hadn't been married or engaged. There was no ex-wife or girlfriend that she or Gloria knew of. Jealousy couldn't be the motivation. Some of his patients probably had husbands or significant others who could have killed him. Surely none would have decided to have their revenge against other former lovers of Ned's.

This couldn't be about scorned lovers.

She stilled. Or maybe it could be.

Who said the murderer was a man? It wasn't confirmed yet that the victims had been sexually assaulted. Was it?

Maybe some woman who'd secretly been in love with Ned had decided to kill him and all his hussies. The term Gloria had used to describe them brought a wan smile to Elizabeth's lips. The realization that she could very well have hit on the answer chased away any hint of humor.

Three women were dead. God only knew who might be next.

"There you are."

Elizabeth looked up at the sound of Gloria's voice. Her lips instantly rose, but the automatic response melted away when her gaze landed on the other woman standing next to her friend.

"Elizabeth, this is Annabelle Ford." Gloria ushered the other woman forward. "Annabelle, Elizabeth Young, my best friend."

Annabelle extended her hand and Elizabeth had little choice but to shake it. The woman's touch was warm and confident, as was her smile.

"It's a pleasure to meet you, Elizabeth. I'm so sorry it has to be under the present circumstances." Her voice wasn't unpleasant, just a little deep. Like that singer, Tracy Chapman.

Elizabeth studied the tall, thin woman for a long moment, wondering who exactly Annabelle Ford was and why she was with Gloria. Her light-brown hair was cut in a fashionably short style that framed her face. Brown eyes that appeared both intelligent and sincere assessed Elizabeth with equal curiosity.

"Nice to meet you, too," Elizabeth eventually remembered to say.

"Did you order already?" Gloria asked as she took a seat next to Elizabeth. Annabelle settled on the opposite side of the table.

"Just coffee." Elizabeth sipped the warm liquid, acutely aware that Annabelle was still scrutinizing her.

When the waitress had taken drink as well as food orders and rushed away Gloria leaned forward and kicked off the conversation. "I don't know what's going on, but after you called I did some thinking."

Elizabeth had called her friend twice in the past twelve hours. Once around midnight after her run-in with MacBride and then again this morning when he got the call that another woman was dead. She and Gloria had decided to move up the meeting they'd planned for dinner this evening. The suspense was getting to both of them. Elizabeth's need to finish up at the loft was the only reason they'd waited this long.

"This can't be coincidence," Gloria went on. She sat back in her seat and shook her head. "My God, three women...all Ned's patients." She inclined her head toward her guest. "That's why I called Annabelle."

Just when Elizabeth was about to ask who Annabelle was, Gloria told her. "Annabelle is—was Ned's attorney."

"And his confidant," Annabelle put in, that husky voice modulated to a discreet level. "I've known Ned since our college days. We shared a great deal. He was an outstanding psychiatrist and a fine man." She fell silent and her gaze grew distant.

For just a second, Elizabeth couldn't help wondering if Annabelle had been one of Ned's lovers, too. When she'd spoken of their relationship, there'd been an intimacy about her tone. But Annabelle didn't strike Elizabeth as Ned's type. Who knew, though? Ned clearly had a voracious and deviant sexual appetite. Admittedly, Elizabeth hadn't quite fit with his type, either. Maybe she and Annabelle had something in common.

"She knew Ned better than any of us," Gloria rushed to add. "On the way here, she told me some very startling secrets about our old friend."

That roused Elizabeth's attention. She propped her arms on the table and leaned into the circle, speaking directly to Gloria. "How about this news-flash? Whoever is doing this may have both of us on his list, as well."

"Precisely," her friend agreed. "This is why we have to do something."

Elizabeth gave her a palms-up gesture. "Do what? I spend half my time looking over my shoulder. I'm scared to death someone is already watching me." She leaned closer still. "I told you what happened last night."

"Someone besides the FBI, you mean?"

This query came from Annabelle. Startled that Gloria had shared this with a stranger, Elizabeth could only stare at the woman.

"Don't be upset, Elizabeth," Gloria urged. "I had to tell her everything. She can't help us if she doesn't know everything."

Where had she heard that before? Mac had used the same line on Elizabeth, but for totally different reasons. She shook herself. When had she started calling him Mac? "Yes," she said bluntly in response to Annabelle's query. "I feel like someone besides the FBI is watching me."

Annabelle patted Elizabeth's hand. Elizabeth stiffened, not quite comfortable talking about this with a stranger.

"I think you might be right." Annabelle looked from Elizabeth to Gloria and back several times as she spoke, her gaze direct, her voice low but firm. "Have either of you heard of the Gentlemen's Association?"

Both shook their heads. Sounded to Elizabeth like a men's club where strippers dominated the menu.

Annabelle sighed. "Well, it's not something you're going to enjoy hearing about, but I feel I must tell you." Her gaze took on a kind of desperate quality. "Ned shared this information in confidence with me, but he's dead now and I'm almost certain it may be crucial to your continued safety."

Elizabeth's nerves twisted into knots. "What is this Gentlemen's Association?"

"A bicoastal group of men, all wealthy professionals much like Ned, for whom life has become tragically boring because they have it all."

She paused as if to measure their reactions.

"They have all the money they could ever wish for, social status, anything they want," she continued. "So the thrill of a challenge, of the hunt is gone." She shook her head sadly. "I watched this very need eat away at Ned. None of his accomplishments were ever enough. His life lacked the primal kind of excitement that comes from a new conquest. That's why he joined this association."

Elizabeth's blood turned to ice when the next logical thought occurred to her. "The videos."

Annabelle nodded. "They make videos of their conquests, each attempting to outdo the other. They shared them via the Internet in private chat rooms for the entire association's viewing pleasure."

Gloria's gaze locked with Elizabeth's. "He did that to us." Her words were scarcely a whisper but filled with the same emotions crashing through Elizabeth.

Anger, humiliation. The feelings almost overwhelmed her, but she fought to maintain her composure. She had to hear all of this. Had to find a way to protect herself. And her friend. "Go on," Elizabeth prompted.

"Once you become a member of the association," Annabelle explained, "there is no turning back. The only way out is death."

Elizabeth felt her face drain of color. "You think they killed him?"

Annabelle nodded grimly. "That's the only logical answer. Ned had a weakness, ladies. He became addicted to these darker needs. The more perverse the better. I believe that addiction cost him his life. The association is responsible for what he became."

"So you mean," Gloria ventured, "they were responsible the same way a drug dealer is for someone who OD's. You don't mean they literally stuck the dagger in his chest?"

Elizabeth winced at her words. No matter how hard she tried she couldn't block those images from her head. The dagger she'd given Ned had been used as the murder weapon. Had someone done that on purpose? To connect her to his murder? That didn't seem possible since she hadn't even told Gloria about the gift.

"I'm not sure," Annabelle said in answer to Gloria's pointed question. "Exclusivity and anonymity are crucial to the association. I worry that Ned had grown reckless and perhaps garnered the wrong sort of attention. Either that or one of his patients discovered what he'd done and decided to stop him."

Worry twisted in Elizabeth's belly. "But what about the women? I doubt they even knew this association exists. Why kill them?"

Annabelle seemed to ponder the question for a moment. "There's always the possibility the two aren't related. However, a few days before his death Ned told me he thought someone was watching him. He feared he'd crossed the line in some way." She shrugged. "I have no idea what he'd done or thought he'd done. I only know he was concerned." She hesitated. "No, he was *afraid.*"

"Oh…my…God," Gloria murmured.

Both Elizabeth and Annabelle stared at her.

"That's why the FBI is involved. We should have known it would be something bigger than his murder."

Sex videos, the Internet. Made sense to Elizabeth. "You could be right."

"Think about it," Annabelle said, picking up the ball and running with it. "If the association thought

Ned's affiliation had been compromised and the FBI had an eye on him, they would certainly want to neutralize any threat to them. What better way than to execute him?"

Elizabeth still had her doubts. "But what about the women?" she repeated.

Silence reigned for what felt like an eternity.

"They must think one of you knows something." Annabelle gave a decisive nod, warming to her theory. "Obviously they're not certain who knows what, so they've decided to take out all of you, one at a time. Or perhaps the other murders are simply to cast suspicion elsewhere. Have the police chasing their tails looking for a serial killer."

"That's crazy!" Elizabeth hadn't meant to sound so vehement but the whole thing was ludicrous. This was real life. Why would some anonymous association risk killing three women over one jerk they'd already taken out of the picture? "The risk is too great. Why would these people risk so much over one weak link?"

"I don't have all the answers," Annabelle admitted with an urgency that struck a chord of dread deep inside Elizabeth. "The only thing I feel certain of is that both of you," she glanced from one to the other again, "are in serious danger."

"What do we do?" Gloria whispered, fear darkening her face.

A stillness settled over Elizabeth as realization dawned with stunning clarity. Annabelle was right. Though this illusive association might not be the threat, someone was. Whether the killer had an agenda that included Ned and the patients with whom he'd carried on an affair or he just wanted to muddy the waters to keep the police off his trail, he might be just getting started. She or Gloria could be next on his kill list.

"There's only one thing we can do."

Gloria and Annabelle looked to Elizabeth, both obviously having reached the same conclusion. Even Annabelle looked as if she feared she might somehow be on that list. Maybe she was. When it came to animal attraction and raw sex, type wasn't always an immediate concern.

"We fight back," Elizabeth stated, feeling the weight of her own words. She'd been there once, had prayed she'd never have to go back, but here she was, eyeball deep in a battle to prove her innocence. And quite possibly to protect her life. "They already think I'm guilty," she continued solemnly. "All they need is one real piece of evidence. If they can't prove I did it, they'll move on to the next likely suspect." Her gaze slid to Gloria's. "Can you prove where you were that night?"

Gloria's eyes widened. "I..." She shook her head.

"I don't know about this association," Elizabeth confessed, "but the police and the feds won't stop until they have someone to prosecute. If not me, then you." She turned to Annabelle. "Or you." She paused, gathering her courage before she said the rest. "The way I see it, the real problem is staying alive until the police either nail someone or we do it for them."

The three simply stared at one another for a minute that became two.

"How could we possibly—"

"That was my thinking," Annabelle interrupted whatever protest Gloria was about to launch. "The one thing we know for certain is that we can't trust anyone else. We have to work together, just the three of us, and solve this mystery." She pressed a hand to her throat. "Our very lives may depend upon it"

Gloria held up both hands. "Wait. Wait. Wait. How are we supposed to do this?"

Before anyone could answer, the waitress arrived with their orders. Elizabeth had pretty much lost her appetite at this point, but she needed energy for work, as well as for what lay ahead where this murder investigation was concerned.

As soon as the waitress had moved on, Annabelle made a suggestion. "We need to know more about this Gentlemen's Association."

Elizabeth laughed. She couldn't help it. It just popped out. She fiddled with her fork to avoid the expectant looks from the other two. "If the FBI can't find enough evidence to take them down and obviously they can't, how are we supposed to?"

It was her turn to insist on a reality check. She'd been thinking more along the lines of checking out everyone who knew or associated with Ned. People right here in New York, not some theoretical organization they couldn't even prove existed.

"My sentiments exactly," Gloria reiterated.

Annabelle sat in silent consideration for a time. "The FBI will be searching his computers, at the office and at home, but they won't find anything."

Apprehension inched its way up Elizabeth's spine. "What do you mean? How do you know what they will or won't find?"

"The association's business is conducted in cyberspace, the Bureau will try tracking where Ned has been, but they won't find anything, because he used a special system for his little hobby."

Elizabeth didn't know much about computers, but she did know that, like a cell phone or a landline, anything a person did on the computer could be traced. Somehow a trail was left. "So where is this system he used?"

She felt her pulse quicken at the idea of bringing down this association. Her stomach pitched a little at the thought that the members of the demented group had likely seen her video. She tamped down the urge to gag. She didn't even want to think about some of the games Ned had prodded her into playing. God, how could she have been so stupid?

"At his office there's a secret room. It was a part of the original architecture—a bomb or storm shelter of some sort. It's like a vault. But when the building was renovated some forty years ago, it was filled in, or at least that's what the blueprints said." Annabelle smiled knowingly. "Apparently the contractor on the job at the time decided to save himself a little money and just boarded it over. Anyway, Ned discovered it when he had the office remodeled a couple of years ago. He decided to make it a vault for his most private files." She sighed as she peered down at her salad. "Eventually he turned it into a media room for his forbidden pleasure."

Elizabeth felt sick. The more she learned about Ned the angrier she grew at herself for being such a fool.

"You've seen it?" Gloria asked, appalled. "This vault room?"

"Well, I haven't actually seen it, but he did tell me about it. He had some sort of shield installed so the room's presence couldn't be detected. It's all quite high tech."

"We have to go there!" Gloria exclaimed, an extra portion of desperation in her voice.

Elizabeth shook her head. "No. We have to go to the authorities." MacBride's image loomed large in her mind. He would know what to do. Maybe she was an even bigger fool than she knew, but she really believed he wanted to find the truth.

"How do we know we can trust the authorities?" Annabelle argued. "What if one or more of them belong to the association? After all, they haven't brought the association down in all this time. I happen to know that Ned has been affiliated with the group for several years now. What's the holdup?" Her fierce gaze cornered Elizabeth. "I'll tell you why—because they're *men.*"

"We can't trust men on this issue," Gloria agreed. "We get the goods on the association and we take it to the press. We could blow the whole thing wide open, then the authorities would have to take action."

"Not we," Annabelle corrected. Again she looked from Gloria to Elizabeth. "His office is certainly being watched. One person slipping past anyone who might be watching will be problematic enough. But all three of us…" She gave her head a brisk shake. "It would never work."

Seemingly endless seconds of tension-filled silence passed as they digested what her assessment meant.

"I would have done this myself as soon as I was notified of Ned's murder, but the police were everywhere," Annabelle said. "I couldn't risk revealing anything to them." Anger etched troubled lines into the features of her face. "I suppose, on some level I wanted to find whoever had done this to him myself."

Elizabeth and Gloria exchanged a look of uncertainty.

"Besides, even if I had been able to get into his office I couldn't have managed," Annabelle went on. "I was in an accident a few years ago. My right shoulder and my left arm were damaged. I have almost no upper-body strength. The hidden door is extremely heavy and there is no automatic opener. Ned explained the mechanism would be too easily detected. The entryway has to be opened and closed manually."

"I'll do it," Gloria offered without hesitation. She nodded. "I can do it."

Elizabeth shook her head. "No. I'm stronger than you. I'll do it"

"I said," Gloria challenged, her Irish temper flaring in those green eyes, "I would do it."

"I'm accustomed to *manual* labor," Elizabeth pointed out. "I know I can do it. If you get in there and then you can't—"

Gloria heaved a sigh of exasperation. "Fine. You do it."

"Time is of the essence," Annabelle reminded them. "We shouldn't waste any. We need to act now."

"Just one question," Elizabeth wondered aloud. "Why did Ned tell you all this? Wasn't it dangerous for him to tell anyone?" She watched Annabelle closely as she responded. Even a repeat fool like her had her boundaries. She'd only just met this woman.

"I'm—was—his attorney. He wanted me to know," her voice faltered and her eyes grew suspiciously bright, "in case something happened to him. Can you imagine a future renovation uncovering his naughty secrets?"

Well, Elizabeth didn't know this Annabelle from any stranger on the street, but she did know Gloria. She trusted Gloria. And if Gloria thought she was okay, then she must be. Besides, what choice did they have? Annabelle knew far more about Ned and his secrets than the two of them put together.

Elizabeth, for one, did not want a future renovation uncovering a video of her in a compromising position.

Brian Novak was not accustomed to being rousted from bed like a common criminal. His money generally bought him a blind eye. But, Mac mused, there was a first time for everything.

"You know, Agent MacBride," Novak said, his hangover obvious in his rusty voice, as well as his disheveled appearance, "my attorney will be calling your superiors first thing tomorrow morning." He reached, for the crystal decanter on the sideboard that served as a bar in his spacious great room. "I'm quite certain there's a law against this type of behavior."

Agent Duncan had worked half the night and all morning to locate Novak, who'd recently moved into a criminally expensive midtown high-rise. Not one of his colleagues or cronies seemed to have his new address, but Mac had his own ideas about that. Finally Duncan had managed to run down the receptionist at Novak's design firm. Being young and new to the firm, she had been more easily intimidated. She'd rolled over on her boss like a playful puppy.

Now, at half-past noon, Mac finally had Novak's attention. He'd asked him where he'd been on the Friday night the doctor was murdered.

Novak took a sip of his whiskey and made a sound of approval before smiling at the question. "You think I killed Ned Harrison?"

What Mac really thought was that Novak had a connection to the Gentlemen's Association, but he hadn't wanted to press his luck by bringing up that theory unless it became absolutely necessary. Right now Novak was the only possible thread they had left on that case, and even that connection was thin. Too thin. Unlike with Harrison, they had no hard proof that tied Novak to the group. Even with Harrison the only true evidence they'd managed to gather in months of work was one intercepted telephone conversation. Mac had clung to that link, knowing Harrison would eventually make another mistake.

Too bad he got himself dead first.

"Yes," Mac said in answer to Novak's question and to the man's utter surprise. "Actually, I do." Duncan waited silently on the other side of the room. He'd learned the first week on the job with Mac not to speak or show any emotion no matter how startled he might be at what he witnessed.

"Please, gentlemen," Novak gestured to the sofa and chairs, "make yourselves comfortable. This discussion could prove interesting."

Mac didn't have any hard evidence connecting the murders of the women to Harrison's death, but, in his gut, he knew they were connected. Harrison's murderer might have been a woman, but a man had killed those women. The preliminaries on the first two victims had confirmed sexual assault. However things started out, the evidence showed the victims had resisted. Surprisingly the killer had left behind seminal fluid, which could ultimately identify him. Mac wondered if Brian Novak was that stupid.

He had dumped Elizabeth, so he must be. That notion seared Mac's brain like a hot blade.

He blinked it away, refused to allow her into his thoughts right now. She had become a distraction he couldn't afford.

Mac took Novak up on his invitation and settled on the sofa. Duncan remained standing near the door. That routine was another thing he'd learned. When two agents attended an interview, one always stood to maintain the subliminal intimidation factor.

"Do you have an alibi or don't you?" Mac asked.

"I was at a party," Novak said smugly. "Ned was supposed to be there, as well, but I guess he ran into a snag, so to speak."

The man's treatment of Elizabeth Young aside, there was something Mac didn't like about Novak. Maybe it was that beach-bum tan or the windblown way he wore his blond hair. Could be the earring or even the blatant way he stared at Mac. From his manner of dress to his posture, the man clearly thought he was God's gift to women. Men, too, Mac decided. He hadn't missed the way Novak sized up Duncan when they arrived. Poor Elizabeth. She hadn't had a chance against a smooth operator like this. A lamb in the crosshairs of a wolf.

Mac clenched his jaw and attempted again to banish her from his mind. For the hundredth time he marveled at just how much difficulty he was having with this case...with *her*.

"I'd say he did," Mac replied, not the least bit amused by the man's gallows humor. "Why don't you give me some names of people who can verify your whereabouts?"

Novak emptied his glass and set it aside. "Certainly."

As Mac jotted down the information, Novak rattled off a lengthy list of names and phone numbers. When Mac had crossed the *t* on the last one, he lifted his gaze to the other man's. "I don't see Elizabeth Young on your list. Aren't you two involved?"

That was the one time since they knocked on the guy's door that Duncan glanced at Mac. Yeah, yeah, he knew the answer to the question. But this bozo didn't know what Mac knew and what he didn't. Truth was, he wanted—no, needed Novak's take on the relationship. What did that make him? A masochist?

"That relationship ended months ago," Novak said with a practiced laugh. "Your people really need to sharpen their investigative skills."

Mac nodded and made another note on his trusty pad that had absolutely nothing to do with Novak or Elizabeth or this case. "And what exactly was the nature of your former relationship?"

Novak took a deep breath and then slouched back on the couch, allowing his shirt to fall open and offering up his well-defined chest for display.

"Well, let's just say I did her a favor." Novak inclined his head. "I gave sweet little Elizabeth the opportunity to grab the brass ring and she went for it. She couldn't wait to get out of that pathetic little dump of a town. I helped her achieve what she wanted and she made it worth my while."

Mac tensed before he could stop himself. Every muscle in his body jolted with the need to pound the hell out of this scumbag.

A knowing smile lifted one side of Novak's mouth as he leaned forward and braced his arms on his knees, his gaze focused intently on Mac. "She's very good."

Fury sent Mac's blood rushing to his head, throbbing there in time with the stampede in his chest. His fingers tightened around the pen as if it were Novak's neck.

"She's always a little hesitant at first," Novak went on, pretending to be oblivious to Mac's reaction. But he knew. He knew and he enjoyed it immensely. "I suppose it has something to do with her devoutly religious upbringing. I was only her second sexual experience. But," he shrugged, "as hard to prime as she is, once you get her started, man, is she hot."

Mac put his pen and paper away and stood, his control was slipping way too fast. "I'll get back to you as soon as I've checked out your alibi."

Novak pushed lazily to his feet and led Mac to the front door, which he opened.

Mac wanted to beat the hell out of him. He'd never in his life wanted to hurt a man over a woman, but he wanted to tear Brian Novak limb from limb.

Duncan was already heading down the corridor to the elevator, but Mac hesitated in the Novak's doorway. "I wouldn't leave town if I were you." His gaze locked with the other man's. "There will be more questions."

Novak leaned against the doorframe as if being visited by the FBI was an every day occurrence. The bastard didn't even have the good sense to be worried.

"Take her, Agent MacBride," Novak said softly, knowingly. "You won't be sorry."

Mac's fingers curled into tight fists of rage, but somehow he held himself back. "Thanks for your cooperation."

He walked away without a backward glance. As angry as he was, the only thing he could think about was that video and the images it held. The way Elizabeth's body moved...the way her lips parted as she struggled toward release. By the time he reached the elevator, he was as hard as a rock from merely thinking about Elizabeth and what Novak suggested.

He stepped into the waiting car and Duncan punched the button for the lobby. "Strange character, huh?"

Mac's only response was a grunt. He couldn't think clearly enough right now for a proper one. Every ounce of blood in his body had raced to his dick.

He had to close his eyes against the truth he wanted to deny.

Novak had seen it. Had rubbed it in.

Mac wanted Elizabeth. He wanted her riding him slow and easy at first, and then hard and fast, her head thrown back in ecstasy. He wanted her touching him, kissing him. He wanted to feel her lips, her tongue on his skin. And then he wanted to take her with such intensity that she wouldn't even remember a jerk like Brian Novak, much less Ned Harrison, when it was over.

He wanted her all to himself.

Suspect or not.

Mac shook himself. He'd lost it. That much was clear. "Duncan, I want you to take the surveillance on Young tonight."

His partner was about to protest but one look at the ferocity in Mac's eyes and he changed his tune. "Sure," he muttered. "Why not?"

"It's the right thing to do," Elizabeth muttered one last time.

Leaving the subway she glanced around again. No sign of the guy who'd been watching her. She'd had a hell of a time, but she was pretty sure she'd given Agent Duncan the slip. If she'd driven her truck, she would never have been able to do it. So she'd parked it in an alley and then disappeared in the subway before the guy realized what she was up to. Then she'd ducked into a group of missionaries while he searched for her in the crowd on the platform. He was so certain she'd gotten on the train that he'd climbed aboard for a second to look for her. When he moved farther down the platform, she'd sneaked aboard the car he'd just checked. She'd watched him search for her as the train took off for its next stop.

Then she'd walked the ten blocks to the midtown brownstone that was Dr. Ned Harrison's office.

It was really dark along this part of the street. Trees and overhanging architecture all but blocked the meager light from the streetlights. But she knew her way with her eyes closed. What a joke. Look at what it had gotten her.

Nothing but trouble.

With the spare key Annabelle had given her now tightly clasped in her hand, Elizabeth slipped into an alley and then down the backside of the row of brownstones. She tried without success to calm her racing heart, to quiet her breathing. What if she was being watched this very minute? She checked the alley in both directions. Nothing.

Keeping close to the wall, she moved toward the rear door that would lead into Ned's offices. Annabelle had explained she had a key because she'd been his attorney. Since he had no surviving family, his attorney would be the person to settle his affairs. Annabelle gave every indication of being just as unsettled by the murders as Gloria and Elizabeth. This kind of aggressive action seemed their only recourse since they had no idea who to trust. Elizabeth ignored the little voice that warned this was all wrong somehow.

She had to do it. If she didn't find a way to exonerate herself, who would? If she could prove the Gentlemen's Association was involved in Ned's death, then she would be free and clear. First, she needed hard evidence.

Taking a deep breath for courage, she pushed away from the concealing security of the shadowed wall and moved to the door. Though there was no exterior light nearby to worry about, there was just enough moonlight to guide her movements. Thank God the police hadn't padlocked his office as they had his apartment. Made sense since his home—not his office—was the scene of the crime.

She had the key inserted into the lock when she heard it.

A footstep...or maybe leaves rustling.

Before she could turn around, a strong arm snaked around her waist. A punishing hand clamped down on her mouth. The scream she tried to deliver died in her throat.

The cologne her attacker wore provoked a jolt of recognition—of dread. His hard body pressed against her backside, his hot breath on her cheek, she tried to jerk away. She twisted to break free, but he only held her more tightly to him.

His lips close enough to touch her skin, he whispered, "I knew it was you."

CHAPTER EIGHT

"Open the door, Liz," he ordered, his voice savage and cold.

Even before he'd used that pet name for her, she'd known it was *him*. An all-too-familiar tremor had quaked through her the instant he touched her...the instant she felt his breath on her skin and she smelled that hideously expensive cologne he wore.

"Let go of me, Brian, or I'll scream!"

He laughed that condescending sound that personified the very essence of his macho mentality. He considered himself above all others, especially her. Why hadn't she seen that when they first met? Why hadn't she picked up on what a bastard he really was?

"So scream," he taunted. "Who's going to hear you?" He reached for the knob, gave it a fierce twist and kicked the door inward. "We're going to talk." Shoving her inside ahead of him, he quickly closed the door behind him.

Elizabeth scrambled to regain the equilibrium she'd lost physically as well as mentally. Too many possibilities for her to choose just one swirled wildly amid the confusion and irritation clouding her ability to reason. Why was he here? What did they have to talk about?

Brian moved to the long table in the center of the dark interior and switched on one of the brass reading lamps. The dim glow pitched the space into long shadows, but she would have been fine without the light. She had firsthand knowledge of every inch of this room. After all, she'd helped decorate these offices just months ago. How else could she have afforded such an exclusive therapist? She'd worked hard to make Ned's suite of offices into everything he'd wanted. This room was no exception.

Ned's professional library. The walls were lined with gleaming mahogany, book-filled shelves. A single conference-style table, also mahogany, surrounded by upholstered armchairs served as the focal point. Built-in brass reading lamps lined the table, four of them altogether. The classic reading lamps gave the room a more intimate ambiance than overhead lighting. Each lamp was accompanied by a granite ashtray. The far corner of the room was equipped with a bar complete with a wine fridge, a state-of-the-art coffeemaker and a small marble sink. A Monet print hung next to a shiny brass rack that held mugs and glasses. The bar offered a wide array of liquors. A humidor stored the finest in imported cigars. Ned had insisted he needed the very best to entertain colleagues and *special* clients.

She'd learned quickly just what *special* meant to him.

Ned Harrison hadn't missed a trick. Whatever he wanted, he got. No matter the cost. He'd once lived in the upstairs portion of the brownstone, but fame had sent him in search of more elaborate housing. Now the rooms above his offices served as mere storage. She wondered briefly if it had all been worth it. Had his primal urges been worth dying for? She'd pretty much concluded that his murder had something to do with those very urges—and the Gentlemen's Association.

Who would ever have suspected? On the outside he'd been all charm and grace and appeared to have the world at his feet. All one had to do to join him in his glorious life was be obedient and submissive to his demands. Yet somehow he'd always managed to make her think it was what *she* wanted. It sickened her now to realize how naive she'd been.

"Sit." Dragging her attention back to the present, Brian motioned to one of the chairs.

He loved tossing out those one-word commands as if she were a dog or other well-trained pet. Hadn't she been exactly that? Brian was no different than Ned. They were both egotistical pigs.

"No thanks," she threw right back at him, folding her arms in defiance.

Those pale-gray eyes, as hard and icy as a frozen lake, gazed relentlessly into hers as he started toward her. She fought the urge to run. She would not let him have his way. Not again. Not ever again.

"I said sit!" He jerked out one of the chairs and clamped a hand on her shoulder and with crushing strength propelled her into the waiting seat.

For the first time since she'd confirmed it was him, fear slithered around her. What was his problem? More importantly, what was he doing here?

Before she could demand some answers, he gave another order. "Tell me what it is you think you know." He propped himself on the edge of the table, positioning himself so that he could look down at her. "I don't want to have to hurt you."

If he'd slapped her, she wouldn't have been any more surprised. As cruel and belittling as Brian could be, she'd never feared him in the physical sense until now. With her heart pumping feverishly and dread dampening her skin, she grabbed back some courage and dredged up an innocent look. "What're you talking about?"

Her heart beating relentlessly against her sternum, she held her breath and prayed he would let it go at that. He smiled, the surface convention utterly sinister. She swallowed. Hard. Was this some sort of game? She'd never seen him like this.

And suddenly she knew.

Brian was a part of this. He was probably a card-carrying member of the Gentlemen's Association as well. God knew he had the penchant for perversion.

"I know what you did, Elizabeth," he said softly, the gentler tone laced with a threatening edge. "The truth is, I don't give a damn that Harrison is dead." He made a sound, half growl, half chuckle. "He took too many chances." Brian reached out to graze her cheek with his fingertips. She flinched, earning herself another of those unnerving smiles.

"I also know how he felt about you," he continued in that same low tone. His fingers trailed down her throat. "He thought you were special. Didn't want to let you go like he should have." His fingers splayed around her throat.

Elizabeth was determined not to let him see her fear. Damn him. "Don't touch me like that." Hard as it was, she maintained eye contact, kept him looking at her so he wouldn't notice her left hand inching its way toward the nearest ashtray.

His evil smile widened. "All you have to do is tell me the secret you're keeping and everything will be fine. I know you know—that's why you're here." The pressure of his fingers increased ever so slightly, raising goose bumps on her flesh. "He wanted you, so I let him have you. But it wasn't easy. You were mine."

She froze, the thoughts screeching to a halt inside her head. "What're you saying?"

"Marrying you wasn't going to change who I am," he went on. "It would've simply provided the kind of image I need. Until I found you, there hadn't been anyone I would have allowed that privilege. I knew you'd never suspect the nature of my true needs." He traced her cheek with the tip of one finger. "As naive as you were, you could still bring me to my knees with that sweet mouth and that hot body."

Fury burned away every other emotion, including the paralyzing fear she'd felt only a second earlier. She tried to draw away from his touch. This was insane. Nothing he said made sense.

"But Ned..." He dropped his hand away and shrugged. "He was obsessed with you. Just watching you at the parties turned him on. He had to have you. What could I do? He was my best friend."

This just couldn't be. She shook her head in denial of what his words meant. "I rarely even saw the two of you speak. How could he have been your best friend? You didn't even come to his funeral!"

"Our relationship wasn't like that," Brian explained. "It was a private bond. A *dangerous* secret just between us." He leaned down, putting his face close to hers, those menacing eyes carrying enough of an arctic blast to form icicles inside her. "Just like the one I know you're keeping from me."

A new thought punched through the pile of others tumbling into her head. "Gloria introduced me to Ned." She shook her head thoughtfully. "She suggested I see him. *Professionally.*" Brian couldn't be right about any of this. "You didn't have anything to do with my relationship with Ned."

Brian stared at her lips now in a way that had once drawn her like a moth to the flame. Abruptly his earlier threat echoed loudly in her ears. He wanted answers—or he would hurt her. She inched her fingers closer to the nearest ashtray.

"I'm the one who told Gloria that seeing Ned would be a good idea for you."

His statement stunned her, stole her breath. Gloria—her best friend, the only person in the world she trusted—was involved in this? Any bravado she'd managed collapsed like a house of cards. "I don't believe you."

He straightened away from her, snapping out of his fixation with her lips. "Well, it's true. I have no reason to lie." He stared down at her once more, impatience registering. "Tell me what you know." When she would have argued, he said, "Careful now, I don't want you to regret anything." Something knowing slid into his expression. "I could always tell the police that I have evidence you killed him."

"I didn't kill him!" How could he say that? He was insane.

"Of course you did."

Her head moved side to side in denial of his ridiculous accusation. "Why would I kill him?"

"Because he wasn't going to let you go, even after you discovered his socially unacceptable appetite and was repulsed by it. He wanted to keep you anyway. We all knew the troubles the two of you were having." That evil smile stretched his lips once more. "You'd be surprised what can be turned into evidence."

The way she'd openly avoided Ned…the argument…God, the dagger. All of it whipped around in her head. The dagger had been a gift from her. Had Brian planted it at the crime scene? Horror gripped her by the throat. Surely he hadn't killed Ned!

"A man should always know when to let go," Brian rambled on. "But Ned refused. I warned him that keeping you would be a mistake. The longer the relationship went on, the more likely you were to discover our secret. Others were concerned, as well. All you have to do is tell me what you saw or heard and we can take care of this now."

Others? Keeping her? Incredulity momentarily overshadowed the fear. This was the twenty-first century. Men didn't *keep* women. And the only appetite she'd known Ned to have was the insatiable one he had for women. He liked to screw around, especially with those who trusted him on a professional level. One woman would never have been enough for him. He knew how to make a woman think she needed him. To make her believe it had been her idea. Elizabeth stilled. But there had been that one secret—the videos. Was that what Brian meant?

She stared up at the man she'd thought she'd known…the man she was supposed to have married. "I don't know what any of this means," she said, praying he'd buy the innocent act. Her fingers finally touched the edge of the cool granite. Anticipation shot adrenaline into her bloodstream. She struggled to keep the tumultuous emotions from her eyes.

"Tell me, Liz." Brian leaned in her direction again. "How did it feel to plunge that dagger into his chest? Was it like the time you stabbed your brother-in-law, or was it all the better knowing you'd sliced straight into his heart?"

"I didn't do it!" The raw, primal sound of her voice startled even her.

"But can you prove it?" he taunted. "Now, tell me what you know," he roared.

Her fingers curled around the lip of the ashtray. "I don't know anything!" She surged upward and slammed the heavy ashtray into the side of his head before he could block the move. He staggered, then crumpled to the floor.

He didn't move.

A trickle of blood bloomed at his hairline along his temple. Fear slammed into her. Her first instinct was to see how badly he was hurt, but her second overrode the momentary lapse in intelligence. She dropped the ashtray and ran.

She had only one thing on her mind—finding Gloria.

Brian couldn't have been telling the truth. She refused to believe that Gloria had betrayed her. Hadn't they both suffered at Ned's hand? Gloria was just as hurt by Ned as she was. She and Gloria were best friends, for God's sake.

Pushing herself to move faster, Elizabeth bounded onto the sidewalk. Brian could regain consciousness any second and chase her down. She felt certain she'd only stunned him. She didn't want to think what he might have had planned for her. But why? What did he have to do with any of this?

How could she not have known he and Ned were close?

What did they have in common? Ned was a psychiatrist. Brian was an architect. At least five years separated them in age. Their tastes in clothing, music, in everything, were worlds apart. She couldn't even imagine what they talked about except sex, obviously.

The Gentlemen's Association.

The realization struck her like a kick to the abdomen. Brian had to have been a part of it. That explained his comment about the others. He'd seen the videos. Renewed horror rushed through her. How many of *their* love-making sessions had Brian videoed? Her knees threatened to buckle. Would this nightmare ever end? All these years she'd felt so sorry for her sister living in hell with an on-again-off-again drug habit and an abusive husband. Now look at her. Elizabeth hadn't fared much better.

She slammed headlong into a brick wall—or what felt like one. Male. Tall. Strong.

Kicking and clawing, she tried to wrench away from the hands grabbing at her, but he was too strong. She couldn't let him get her now. Had to get away. She opened her mouth to scream.

"Stop fighting me!" he ordered.

Recognition filtered through her hysteria. She went limp and her gaze flew to his face.

MacBride.

"What the hell are you running from?"

In the next second Elizabeth realized two things.

She had just committed assault and been caught fleeing the office of a victim in an ongoing murder investigation.

A murder investigation in which she was the prime suspect.

Her life was over.

MacBride shook her just hard enough to get her attention. Those strong fingers gripping her arms sent spears of heat firing through her. "What happened, Elizabeth? What're you doing?"

"I...I thought I'd left something in the library." She felt uncomfortable at the idea of having to lie to him again. She was tired of lying—especially to him. If he ever found out...

Even in the dim light she saw his eyes narrow. "At Harrison's office?"

MacBride was no fool. He knew exactly where she'd been. Had probably known this was where she was headed the minute his man reported her having given him the slip in the vicinity of midtown.

"Yes." She sucked in a ragged breath and shrugged free of his hold, even though a part of her would have liked nothing better than to wilt into those powerful arms. "I helped decorate his office," she stammered, grappling for an acceptable excuse, "and I only just realized my paint chips were missing. I thought maybe I'd left them there."

"The work you did for Harrison was months ago, wasn't it?"

She lifted her chin and flat out ignored his innuendo. "I didn't miss them until I needed them."

He cocked his head and eyed her suspiciously. "That doesn't explain why you were running for your life. Was someone else there, too?"

God almighty. If by some sick twist of fate Brian was dead, she was done for twice over. Even if he was alive and still hanging around, she didn't want MacBride to talk to him. The last thing she needed was Brian putting ideas about evidence and motives into MacBride's head. She was already at the top of his go-to-jail list.

"While I was searching I," her mouth worked but a plausible excuse momentarily escaped her, "I thought I heard someone outside. I got spooked so I ran." She held her breath as she waited for his reaction to the enormous fabrication.

"I guess we should check it out, then."

Before she could come up with a reason not to go back, he was dragging her toward Ned's office. At the door her heart leaped into her throat. If Brian opened his big mouth…

"You left the door open?"

The door stood ajar just as she'd left it but there was no sign of Brian. She blinked and looked again. No Brian. Thank God.

She nodded in answer to MacBride's question. "I was too scared to take the time to lock up." Now that was the truth. She spotted the ashtray on the floor under the conference table. She prayed MacBride wouldn't notice. At least there wasn't a big puddle of blood on the floor.

"You have a key?" A dash of surprise colored MacBride's voice.

"I guess I forgot to give it back after the job was done," she offered, moving to the conference table to lean against it. She couldn't trust her ability to stay vertical at the moment and she hoped to block his view of the granite ashtray. A mixture of relief and trepidation had turned her muscles rubbery.

Brian must have noticed that someone had detained her as she fled. He'd likely slipped away unnoticed in the other direction.

Lucky him.

She was stuck here with MacBride.

Not that being stuck with him was such a hardship. At least he didn't want to kill her…and he was hot. *Really?* She did a mental eye roll. No matter that there was a definite attraction between her and the Bureau's hotshot agent, she did not need any additional complications right now. Not to mention the fact that MacBride thought she was a killer.

She still had trouble accepting that Ned was actually dead—murdered. She'd never known anyone who wound up murdered. Setting aside the fact that in some ways he'd deserved a bad end, he'd still been a human being and now he was gone.

Standing here in the library she'd helped choose colors and carpeting for, the reality crashed in on her. No force on earth could bring Ned back. His life was over and hers might very well be, too, if MacBride had anything to say about it. Not to mention Brian was into something she wasn't sure she wanted to understand. She really needed to talk to Gloria.

"You're certain there was no one else here besides you?"

Elizabeth snapped back to attention. Careful not to look directly at him, she nodded. "Just me—until

I heard the sound outside. Someone must have been poking around in the alley." She would let him draw his own conclusions. Could have been a homeless person for all MacBride knew.

He bent down and picked up something from the floor. "I guess I overlooked this the last time I was here." He held the item out for her inspection and she knew instantly what it was. Brian's money clip. A fourteen-carat gold showpiece with the initials BWN. Brian Wade Novak.

MacBride dropped the item into his jacket pocket. "I'll just take it in for analysis."

If he questioned Brian...

MacBride's slow, deliberate approach abruptly derailed that worrisome thought. She tried not to look at him, but she simply couldn't help herself. The way he moved, fluid, predatory. The fit of that expensive suit, even with his collar unbuttoned and his tie jerked loose, lent a dangerous element. There he was all polished and smart-looking on the outside, but something deeply primal simmered just beneath those outer trappings. She could see it in his blue eyes. She could feel it vibrating all around him like a force field. That short, silky hair looked as if he'd just raked his fingers through it, and his jaw sported a five o'clock shadow.

Everything about him screamed sex, blatantly challenged any female within sight to come have a taste.

He stopped no more than two feet away, his long-fingered hands propped firmly on his hips, the lapels of his jacket pushed aside. She told herself not to look into those eyes, not to let him draw her in more deeply. Then he spoke and any hope of denying the urge was lost.

"This was not a smart move, Elizabeth," he said quietly, his voice soft and deadly serious. "Coming here makes you look even guiltier than you already do. Didn't you stop to consider that access to this office was too easy? I've had someone watching twenty-four/seven for just this moment. You'd better start talking and this time I want the truth."

She blinked once, twice, her mind frantically attempting to focus on his words while the part of her that made her female zeroed in on all that marked him male. Her very skin felt electric, ready to combust "I told you I—"

"I know what you told me, but it was a lie. Just like the other lies you've told me. I'm giving you another chance here. Tell me what you know, and this will be a lot easier on the both of us."

Summoning her scattered resolve, she looked him square in the eye and said the only thing she could. "I don't know what you want from me, Agent MacBride. I've told you everything I know."

"Did you have sex with Harrison the night he was murdered?" he asked casually, unhurriedly. He might pretend to be relaxed but he gave himself away when he shifted his gaze from hers, a visible concession to the tension mounting between them.

"No," she said adamantly.

"Then you won't mind submitting a sample for DNA comparison to the intimate body hair discovered at the scene."

Mac knew he'd gotten her attention then. He heard the harsh intake of breath, saw the widening of her eyes.

"My attorney—"

"Your attorney can't make this go away, Elizabeth," he cut in smoothly. "Only I can. To do that I need to be able to eliminate the possibility that you were in Harrison's bed that night."

For an instant she wavered, uncertain. He didn't want that moment of increased vulnerability to pass. "Making that elimination would be a major step in the right direction."

"I guess it couldn't hurt," she said stiffly.

He watched her lips as she spoke, knowing it was a mistake and somehow unable to help himself. There was just something about her mouth, something that drew him, made him want to taste her. Made him want those lips on his body...ravishing him the way she had Harrison in that damned video he couldn't get out of his head.

Before he could thwart the impulse, he'd moved closer, his thigh brushing hers as he stood closer than was safe. The resulting charge went straight to his groin, hardened him instantly.

"See how easy that was?" he offered roughly, fighting to stay on track.

She watched his lips now, her own slightly parted. Was she attracted to him, as well, or was this just one of her maneuvers to distract him?

Her tongue darted out to moisten her lips. Control slipped another notch and he was pretty sure that getting any *harder* would be impossible. He had her right where he wanted her. He couldn't let the moment go—just yet.

"Tell me why you really came here tonight," he urged, his voice as soft as it was insistent. "Was it Novak's idea or yours?"

Her gaze collided with his. "I'm no fool, Elizabeth. The clip has his initials on it. And I told you I had someone watching." The agent on surveillance had somehow missed anyone except Elizabeth. His instincts told him Novak had been here and Mac trusted his instincts above all else.

"It's..." She shook her head. "It's not what you think."

"How do you know what I think?"

She lifted one shoulder, confusion and uncertainty haunting her eyes. "You think I killed Ned."

For the first time since he'd met Elizabeth Young, he allowed himself to look at her—the woman, not the suspect. The tomboyish sprinkle of freckles across the bridge of her nose. The way her glasses always needed pushing up or setting straight. The rich amber color of her eyes. His fingers itched to tangle in the thick mass of dark hair she always kept pulled back in a braid or ponytail. Long strands had slipped loose now. They clung to her face, appearing even darker against the creaminess of her skin. But it was her mouth that tormented him more than anything else. Wide, full, the bottom lip noticeably heavier than the top.

"You wanted to kill him," he said without thinking.

She chewed that tempting lower lip for a second. "But I didn't."

"Was Novak in on it? Did the two of you plan this together?"

That sent her rushing for cover, but he blocked her path. "He was, wasn't he?"

"I don't know!" She tried to push away the arm that held her back, but only succeeded in shoving him a little further over the edge with her touch.

"Is he involved with the Gentlemen's Association, too?"

Her head came up. She opened her mouth to refute his suggestion, but her face gave her away before she could tell him yet another lie.

"Don't waste your breath, Elizabeth. Your eyes already provided the answer I suspected." He choked out a laugh. "Do you have any idea how much danger you're in right now?"

The fear and uncertainty vanished with one blink of her long-lashed lids. "From who? Them or you? You keep pushing me and pushing me like you really believe I'm guilty, but I see the way you look at me. I'm not blind, MacBride."

And that easily he was lost. He took her face in his hands. As his mouth swooped down to claim hers, he felt the little hitch in her breathing. She tensed but didn't draw away. He took that as permission to plunder the luscious mouth that had been driving him insane for days.

That was the final rational thought Mac managed. She tasted like chocolate and coffee. And she was hot, so damned hot.

He gently lifted her glasses up and off, leaving them on the table so that he could get back to touching her with both hands. His fingers delved into the thick softness of her hair, and he groaned with satisfaction. He'd wanted to touch her like this from the moment he first laid eyes on her. Or maybe before… when he'd watched that video over and over. He took the kiss deeper, thrusting his tongue inside her, wanting, needing more than he dared take.

She held back, refused to surrender to the kiss. He was kissing her. She allowed it but didn't respond.

Images of the innately sexual creature on the video flooded his head, and a jolt of jealousy went through him. He wanted her like that, wanted her responding to his touch, to his kiss.

He kissed her harder, demanding a reaction.

And that made him just like Novak…and the others.

He tore his mouth from hers, but couldn't draw away completely at first. He had to hover there. Close enough to feel her pull. He licked his lips, tasting her, feeling her quick little puffs of warm breath on his damp skin. The way she smelled, like a rose beneath the warm sun, made him want to pull her to him again.

But he didn't.

He stepped back, at a loss for words to explain himself. She refused to look at him, kept her gaze somewhere in the vicinity of the fourth button of his shirt. Right about the same location where the knife had entered Harrison's chest. Another dose of reality slammed into him.

"I'll take you home."

At some point he would need to acknowledge having overstepped his bounds. Not right now.

Right now walking away pretty much took all the strength he possessed.

CHAPTER NINE

Elizabeth lay in the predawn darkness and mulled over the previous night. A part of her had wanted to go to Gloria's place and demand answers. How could she do that? It would be an outright admission that she didn't trust her friend. A slap in the face. She just couldn't do it. Gloria was the one person she *had* been able to trust. Brian had to be lying. There was no other explanation. Ned had almost ruined hers and Gloria's friendship. It would be just like Brian to try and finish it off.

He was jealous that way. A selfish son of a bitch who cared only for himself.

She closed her eyes and exhaled a heavy breath. She'd been so blind. The whole idea of moving to the big city, of working with the masters at a design firm like Design Horizons. It had been her dream since she was twelve, when she realized what one could do with a mere gallon of paint and a yard of fabric. Her father's work as a handyman had ingrained in her a love of houses. Big, small, old or new. She loved bringing them to life with color. As she'd grown older she realized there was a whole world of possibilities out there beyond her little hometown. Though she'd had no formal training or education in the field, she was good at designing and decorating interiors. Really good. Her skill came naturally, like breathing. She looked at a room and saw a blank canvas.

The break with Brian had ended all that. She had no reputation, no contacts of her own, so she'd had to fall back on the sort of work she could do without any of those things—good, honest hard work. Interior painting could be backbreaking. You had to be good, as well as fast, to earn a living wage with little more than a brush and a roller. She was both, but she was a woman, which was an automatic strike against her. She'd had to work cheaply at first, and being choosy about her work location hadn't been an option. Finding Boomer had proved a lucky break. He wasn't afraid of anything, including hard work.

Now her work was relatively steady. The locations were a great deal better and she'd earned the beginnings of an excellent reputation. She could make it.

Just when things had been looking up financially, if not personally, Ned had entered the picture. Sure, she'd seen him around. The kind of parties Brian attended or hosted catered to the rich and socially privileged. Seeing Ned on a professional level had felt right at first. He'd seemed kind. She'd needed that. All her life everyone she'd depended on or needed had deserted her, one way or another. Her mother had walked out on them when Elizabeth was in kindergarten, her father had died last year, and then Brian had dumped her. According to Ned, the panic attacks were caused by years of uncertainty and stress. His counseling had helped.

The affair had been an accident—at least she'd thought so at the time. Brian's caustic words reverberated in her head. It was hard to believe that Ned would have set out to reel her in like that when he could have had any woman he wanted. The memory of the video slammed into her thoughts like an out-of-control dump truck on a downhill stretch. She shouldn't be shocked at anything she discovered about him. Worse, she kept referring to the video in the singular sense when the truth was she had no idea how many Ned had made or if Brian had done the same.

Bastards.

She flopped over onto her side. But the part about Gloria, she simply refused to believe it was true. Elizabeth had every intention of chalking that one up to Brian's cruel selfishness. He'd lost his friend and he wanted Elizabeth to lose hers. The first time she'd gotten accolades from a pleased design client, Brian had found a way to ruin it. Despite all the nasty little things he'd done, she hadn't realized until the very end just how selfish he was. Or maybe she hadn't wanted to see the truth.

But that was over now and she was left wondering if Brian was involved in Ned's murder. Had it been his intent to set Elizabeth up? The fact that whoever had killed Ned had used the dagger she'd given him seemed to support that theory. Had Ned bragged to Brian about her gift? She considered MacBride's suggestion that she submit to DNA testing. The implication made her curl into the fetal position. She didn't kill Ned, so she wasn't really worried on that score. On the other hand, what if whoever had attempted to set her up had planted the evidence the police had discovered?

A harsh laugh burst from her. *Okay, Elizabeth, exactly how would someone have gotten any of your pubic hair without your knowledge?*

Hold up. It wasn't such an outlandish idea. Hair came off in the tub and on the bathroom floor when she used a brush or dried herself after a shower.

Sometimes there were loose hairs scattered about when she got around to housework and laundry. Someone could have come into her place while she was at work and Mrs. Polk was off playing bridge or visiting her old lady friends. It wasn't outside the realm of possibility. Nor was the possibility that Brian had saved a couple of her hairs from their time as a couple. They'd lived together for several months.

The entire concept was just too surreal. That kind of thing only happened in movies.

This wasn't a movie. This was real. Elizabeth hugged her knees more tightly to her chest. MacBride was certain she was involved or knew something important. He knew she was not telling him everything. He read her so well. And he kissed her like no one had ever kissed her before.

Her skin heated from the inside out. She'd tried so hard to block the memory, but it just wouldn't go away. All night she'd awakened every couple of hours, and her first thought each time was of his kiss, his touch. He'd startled her with the move, although some part of her had known it was coming, and she'd frozen, unable to respond on even the most basic level.

Who was she kidding? She always froze—at first. It took a great deal of trust just to dive in, and she simply didn't trust any man that much. She'd trusted her father, but he was gone now, then she'd put her faith in Brian, and look where that had gotten her. Her sister had trusted her husband and she'd paid dearly for it. So had Elizabeth. She'd almost gone to prison after taking that knife to her brother-in-law to stop the son of a bitch. Hadn't it been another man who'd taken their mother away from them? She'd fallen so desperately for the guy she'd deserted her husband and two small children, never to be heard from again.

Ned had explained it was that abandonment that had set the stage for Elizabeth's current phobia. She wasn't entirely sure that was true, since she'd long ago blocked all thought of her mother. Maybe on some level it was true.

One thing was certain, she couldn't trust MacBride. He was an FBI agent who considered her a suspect in his current investigation. Even if she could muster up the courage to trust him, he would use that trust to prove her guilty.

No matter how attracted she was to him—and she was definitely attracted—she couldn't let down her guard. Ned had offered some fancy name for her little trust issue, but she didn't necessarily agree with his conclusion. Sure, with a guy she was attracted to she could work up enthusiasm for sex eventually—*eventually* being the key word. She closed her eyes and pressed her forehead to her knees. Brian had called her frigid. They'd fought so many times over her lack of sexual ambition that eventually she'd learned to submit to his needs a little more quickly, but only with conscious effort. Ned had known all the right words to coax her into cooperation. But no one, absolutely no one, had ever made her *want* to jump in with both feet.

Except MacBride.

Oh, she'd gone through the usual routine of freezing up at his first touch. Yet, in mere seconds she'd wanted to throw her arms around him and climb his hard male body. The only thing that had stopped her had been that damned lack of trust. Still, for the first time in her life, she was certain she could have dived straight in, ignoring the whole trust issue. Just her luck to find the one man who set her on fire with barely a touch and he wanted to charge her with murder.

She uncurled and rolled onto her back to stare at the ceiling, noting the cracks in the old plaster and the fact that the ceiling, as well as the rest of her apartment, needed a fresh coat of paint. She harrumphed. Painters were like hairdressers. They always needed a makeover but were too busy taking care of everybody else to find time to do their own. That was the story of her life. Always wishing for what she couldn't have.

Her cell rang, cutting short the self-pity session.

Her heart took a breath stealing dip. It was scarcely daylight. Who would call her at this hour? Her sister? Something could have happened to one of the kids. She snatched the phone from the bedside table. Didn't recognize the number. "Hello."

"Elizabeth?"

Not immediately able to identify the woman's voice, Elizabeth frowned. Something like a moan and then a grating attempt at clearing a throat echoed across the line. "Yes," Elizabeth ventured.

"Elizabeth, it's Annabelle."

The ache of hopelessness in the woman's voice propelled Elizabeth into a sitting position. Fear ripped through her at her first thought—Gloria. "What's wrong?"

"There's been another murder."

Elizabeth went numb.

"I heard the call go out on the police scanner," Annabelle explained solemnly. "I checked the address they called out against Ned's patient log."

A tense beat of silence sent Elizabeth's heart into warp speed.

"It's Marissa Landon, it has to be." Another of those moan-like sounds. "Is this ever going to stop? Why can't the police do something?"

"I'll call Gloria." Elizabeth scarcely recognized the stone-cold voice as her own. Thank God it wasn't Gloria. But still, another woman was dead... *murdered*.

"We have to talk," Annabelle urged. "I think there's a new pattern developing here. Did you get to Ned's office yet?"

Elizabeth was already out of bed and searching for clothes. The question stirred the dread that had settled like a rock in her stomach. "We can talk about that when we're all together. Where should we meet?"

"My office." She gave Elizabeth the uptown address. "I'll be waiting."

After disconnecting, Elizabeth punched in Gloria's number and jumped into her clothes as she waited out the rings.

Four murders. Ned had been dead for just over two weeks and already four of his patients were dead.

Dear God, who would be next?

Mac was at the office when the call came in. He hadn't been able to sleep, so he'd come in to dissect what he had on the murders that had been dubbed the *Socialite Murders*, since all the victims had been Manhattan society elite.

All three of the women were young, all were beautiful and wealthy, but other than that the only true connection among them was that they'd been patients of Ned Harrison. After the second murder, Brannigan had started checking female victims against Harrison's patient log as a matter of course. Each victim had been bound to her bed and gagged with a pair of her own panties. The ritual was the same each time—she was sexually assaulted and then murdered with a single slash to the throat. No sign of a struggle in any room other than the bedroom where the victim was found. Who was this man that the women would allow him into their homes without question? Did he force his way in with a gun?

At each scene numerous prints were lifted, but it would take forever to crosscheck them all. The killer's seminal fluid was left behind in each case. DNA testing and cross-matching with CODIS—the FBI's databank of DNA profiles on convicted offenders—as well as any other available databanks was in the works. Mac had made the necessary calls to hopefully prompt a speedy response on the DNA results.

Now there was a fourth victim. It wasn't that Mac hadn't anticipated additional victims. Unfortunately, he had. Whether Brannigan was ready to admit it or not, this was the work of a serial killer and somehow the killings were connected to Harrison. Being a current patient of the deceased psychiatrist and a star in one of his sex videos appeared to be the common links. NYPD would have its hands full warning the potential victims as well as offering some level of protection to those who needed it.

The one thing about the latest killing that startled the hell out of Mac was the location. The victim was found in her home less than six blocks from Harrison's office—where both Elizabeth and Novak had been the night before. According to the ME she'd been dead long enough to be in full rigor mortis, which indicated the victim had been dead twelve to fourteen hours.

Mac glanced at the digital clock on his desk as he prepared to head to the crime scene. It was seven now. That would, roughly speaking, put the time of death at sometime between five and seven the previous evening. He'd discovered Elizabeth and evidence of Novak at Harrison's office at approximately seven-thirty. He was still furious that the surveillance team monitoring Harrison's office had somehow missed Novak's presence. They'd spotted Elizabeth and called him immediately, but they'd missed Novak entirely. The wily bastard couldn't be that good. Catching someone with motivation to get inside Harrison's office had been the whole point of surveillance versus locking down the damn place. They needed a break in this case. With the proper surveillance he could have pinpointed Novak's exact time of arrival. Hell, maybe he'd just beat it out of the guy.

Mac was still investigating Novak, but there were several things he already knew about the man. He'd been born to wealthy parents who were still movers and shakers in the financial world. His father had been immensely disappointed when his only son chose to go into architecture and design rather than mergers and takeovers. Novak had never been in any real trouble, other than one petty drug bust in college and a charge four years ago of soliciting. Like Harrison, Novak had a sick little obsession with the seamier side of sex.

Until now Mac hadn't had any evidence to warrant the subpoena of DNA evidence from either Novak or Elizabeth, but things were different now. They had both been in the vicinity of the crime, were guilty of breaking and entering at the office of a recent murder victim whose case was ongoing, and the two were definitely hiding something.

One way or another, Mac intended to know what that something was.

He would push Elizabeth until she broke.

Before he could stop it, the memory of kissing her erupted inside him, yanking the rug right out from under him and sending his senses reeling all over again. He'd worked hard every waking moment since that damned kiss not to think about her that way or to recall the taste of her lips. To forget the insane move he'd made kissing her. But he couldn't seem to keep it pushed away. The taste of her, the smell of her, kept haunting him.

He shook his head as he exited his office and headed for the elevators. He couldn't stop thinking about her when what he needed to be focusing on was the facts.

Fact one: Elizabeth Young was supposed to meet Ned Harrison the night he was murdered.

Fact two: the murder weapon was a gift from Elizabeth.

Fact three: an illicit affair between Elizabeth and Harrison had ended badly. Already several of their mutual friends had given statements to that effect.

Fact four: Elizabeth had a record of drug possession and felony assault, with a knife no less.

Fact five: she had no alibi for the night of Harrison's murder.

Finally and the most damning of all: Elizabeth knew he was attracted to her. She'd said as much. *I see the way you look at me.* Which meant he wasn't being objective where she was concerned.

Even in light of all those glaring facts he still wanted her. The idea that she could have been the one murdered last night when she'd given his partner the slip turned his blood cold.

He was in trouble here.

Elizabeth sat adjacent to Gloria in one of the matching wing chairs flanking Annabelle's desk. The office was nice, not quite as luxurious as Ned's, but on that order. She had an uptown address that spoke of money and prestige.

Elizabeth had no idea what kind of attorney Annabelle was, since she hadn't met her until yesterday, but if accommodations were any indicator, she must be doing well for herself. Elizabeth appreciated any time a woman could flourish in a man's world.

"Look at the last names." Annabelle pointed at the list she'd made of the victims, all former patients of Ned's.

"Damn," Gloria breathed the word. "They're in alphabetical order."

Annabelle nodded in confirmation. "Adele, Bumbalough, Fowler and now Landon. I checked the log of patients and there are four more, including the two of you."

Elizabeth scrubbed at the frown creasing her forehead. "I'm sure Ned had a lot more than eight patients."

"Certainly," Annabelle hastened to agree. "These are merely the ones who were or had been his patient during the past year, and who shared a more personal relationship with him."

Elizabeth and Gloria exchanged uncertain glances.

Annabelle sighed. "Yes, I'm aware that Ned sometimes broke the rules with his patients." She folded her hands atop the clean blotter on her desk. "I didn't really have a problem with his less-than-savory involvement with the association and the darker side of sexuality." She paused, her expression intent, thoughtful. "But I fear this association and crossing the line with his patients delved into far more dangerous territory than he intended."

"How did you figure out which patients he was *involved* with?" Elizabeth swallowed tightly.

Annabelle leaned back in her chair and fixed her gaze on Elizabeth. "To be perfectly honest with you, I suspected what was going on months ago."

"What did you do?" Gloria seemed to steel herself in anticipation of her answer.

"I confronted him, of course. Gave him my professional opinion whether he wanted to hear it or not."

"But he didn't want your advice," Elizabeth said, knowing how Ned would have reacted to being told what to do by anyone. He was far too arrogant to allow anyone to rule any aspect of his world.

Annabelle looked down for a moment before saying more. "He was my friend," she said when she again met their gazes once more. "I didn't agree with what he did, but I couldn't just walk away, either."

Elizabeth blinked back the tears that blurred her vision. Ned had used them all. Furious with herself, she glanced at her cell. Nine-thirty already. Boomer would be wondering where she was. He knew to get started without her, but she couldn't put off leaving for the job site much longer. Getting behind wasn't an option. She needed to fulfill this contract. She needed the money.

"Did you find the hidden door?"

The unexpected question startled Elizabeth back to attention. With the news of another murder, she'd completely forgotten about the previous evening's mission, even though she'd promised Annabelle an update and had expected the question.

She shook her head. "Brian followed me there or stumbled upon me there, and I couldn't do anything."

Annabelle straightened, clearly surprised. "Brian Novak?"

Elizabeth nodded. "He..." She frowned, trying to remember his exact words. "He accused me of killing Ned and then urged me to tell him what I know." Her gaze connected with Annabelle's. "Do you think he was talking about the Gentlemen's Association?"

"Brian was watching Ned's office?" Gloria asked, her voice, as well as her expression, revealing her shock.

"Apparently." Elizabeth couldn't think of any other explanation for why he was there at precisely the same time she was. The whole encounter had been way creepy. "He kind of scared me." As furious as it made her that MacBride had her under surveillance, the sight of that nondescript sedan parked outside her place this morning had been reassuring. It hadn't been him, but it was one of his men.

"Jesus," Gloria muttered on a shaky breath. "This just gets more bizarre by the minute."

"I certainly can't hazard a guess what Novak had on his mind, but I think we can all surmise that if the police don't stop this murderer..." Annabelle allowed her words to trail off. She didn't have to say the rest.

"What're we going to do?" Gloria looked from Annabelle to Elizabeth. "If there're only four others and two of them are us, we have to do something to protect ourselves."

Her friend was right, Elizabeth agreed silently, dread slithering through her. Gloria was her friend, her best friend. She wasn't about to put any stock in anything Brian said. She trusted Gloria. To confront her with Brian's accusations would be wrong. "How do we do that? And what about the other two women?"

"Do you have someone you could stay with at night?" This from Annabelle. She looked from one to the other. "I really don't think either of you should be alone, especially at night." She massaged her temples as if an ache had begun there. "I can't believe the police haven't noticed this already. They're supposed to be trained to see these details. You should have police protection."

Elizabeth wondered if Annabelle would count FBI surveillance? Probably wasn't what she meant. MacBride wasn't trying to protect Elizabeth, not really. *Because he thinks you're a murderer.* Deep inside, where no one else could see, she felt off center... completely off balance.

"I could stay with my sister," Gloria said uncertainly. "She has her husband's gun."

This time the tremble stayed with Elizabeth. "That's a good idea," she said thinly, trying hard to be steady.

"Elizabeth, you could stay with us, too," Gloria urged.

Elizabeth shook her head. If the killer was after her, no way would she endanger Gloria's family. She stilled. What if it was her he really wanted? What if all these other murders were nothing but a decoy? She could be the coup de grace.

Enough Elizabeth. Don't make this about you. It's about Ned…somehow.

"I'll ask Boomer to stay over." That would work. He'd be glad to. And he was tough. She wouldn't have to worry with him around. "Besides, the feds are still watching me"

"I don't trust your safety to them," Gloria said, her voice still full of apprehension. "Getting Boomer to stay with you is a good idea. I don't think any of us should be alone." She looked at Annabelle. "What about you?"

The attorney waved her hands in a forget-about-it gesture. "I'll be fine. I have friends I can stay with. So you'll be with your sister," she said to Gloria, "and you'll have *Boomer* to protect you?" She frowned. "Who exactly is Boomer?"

Elizabeth laughed, the quick burst of humor easing some of the tension choking her. "He's my assistant."

"An ex-con," Gloria added. "She'll be safe with him."

Annabelle looked a little skeptical, but said, "No doubt." She gave a nod of finality. "I'll also come up with a legitimate reason to contact the other two women on the list and warn them as best I can."

Until that moment Elizabeth hadn't really felt comfortable with Annabelle but her determination to help had won Elizabeth over. Another scenario nudged at her though she was sure the police had considered this one already. "Annabelle, could Ned have been murdered for his money?"

The attorney weighed the question for a moment.

"I don't see how. I've started his will through probate. His brother was to inherit everything—"

"His brother?" Gloria asked incredulously. "I didn't know he had any siblings."

Annabelle's expression turned solemn. "Well, he did have a brother, but he died several years ago. With no other family, in accordance with Ned's wishes, his assets will be distributed to various charities."

Well, well, Elizabeth pondered. Who would have thought that Casanova Ned would turn into a philanthropist upon his death? Too bad he hadn't shown that kind of compassion in life. She'd never once wondered if he had any family. He just seemed to *be*—as if he'd sprung forth fully grown with no need for any family.

All of them had work to get to, so the meeting adjourned and Gloria and Elizabeth walked out together. On the sidewalk Gloria, in vintage Gloria fashion, hailed the first cab that passed. At least a dozen always whizzed by Elizabeth before she could get one's attention.

"Call me tonight," Gloria ordered as she climbed in. "I want to hear Boomer's voice coming across your phone."

Elizabeth nodded. "Don't worry. I won't take any chances. And you'll be at your sister's, right?"

"Immediately after work," Gloria assured her. The look in her eyes told Elizabeth there wasn't any question. Gloria was as afraid as she was.

When Gloria's taxi had merged with the traffic, Elizabeth walked slowly toward the garage where she'd parked her truck. Other pedestrians in a hurry to get to work brushed past her, and she moved closer to the curb to avoid them. She thought about the woman who'd been murdered last night and tried without success to understand why this was happening. Why would anyone want to kill Ned's patients unless he somehow suspected one of them of being responsible for Ned's death? And that was assuming the murderer was a friend of Ned's.

Is that how Brian fit into all this? Had he killed Ned because of her? She shook her head. Brian didn't care that much about anyone and neither did Ned. Playing sick little games appeared to be what the two had in common. Could their game playing have turned into murder? How did the Gentlemen's Association fit into the puzzle? Were all these women being murdered because someone thought they knew his secret?

If the killer had a list, Elizabeth was certainly on it. If he knew about her fight with Ned and the visit to his apartment, was she the ultimate target? If that was true, why kill the others? Maybe he wasn't sure and just wanted to be absolutely certain he got the right one.

She'd lived with Brian for months. Surely she would know if he were capable of murder. Then again, after what she'd witnessed last night she wasn't so sure.

A car screeched to a halt at the curb, the abrupt sound jerking Elizabeth back to the here and now. Her heart slammed mercilessly against the wall of her chest and she readied to run.

Would he strike in broad daylight on a crowded street?

The emblem on the sedan registered and Elizabeth stalled. Her relief was so profound that her knees almost buckled. The passenger window lowered and MacBride peered at her from inside the dark sedan. She'd forgotten all about her private watchdog.

"Get in," he ordered.

Elizabeth waited as a couple of pedestrians pushed past her, rushing for a slowing cab. As soon as the last of her fear had subsided, irritation instantly replaced it. "What do you want?" she demanded as she stepped nearer to the curb and his waiting car.

"Get in," he repeated, his gaze every bit as fierce as his command.

She leaned down to peer inside the car. "Why?" she asked, uncomfortable with his whole demeanor. As grateful as she was at this point to have him watching her, she could do without the attitude.

"Get in willingly or I'll arrest you. It's your choice."

The edge in his voice sliced right through her annoyance, shifting it to uneasiness. "If you insist."

Elizabeth opened the door and slid into the passenger seat. Before she had time to fasten her seat belt he barreled into the flow of traffic, earning himself squealing tires and impatient honks.

"I'm only going to ask you this once, Elizabeth," he said without glancing her way. "What were you and Novak doing at Harrison's office last night?"

Not that again. "We argued the way we always do. Satisfied?" He didn't look at her, which she could blame on traffic, but his stony profile warned there was more trouble and it had her name written all over it.

"Did he leave Harrison's office before or after you?"

She held her breath, fought the urge to tell him everything. She couldn't. She wanted to trust him. Dammit. *Can't.* "I left first. What difference does it make?"

"Because around that time, just a few blocks away from where I found you, Marissa Landon was being murdered."

CHAPTER TEN

Mac drove for almost ten minutes without speaking. Elizabeth's tension escalated with every passing second. She felt certain he planned to take her to his office, but he didn't. Then she figured he planned to take her to the police station to face those two detectives again, Brannigan and the partner whose name she couldn't recall. He didn't do that, either.

Instead, he drove, finally stopping in front of a well-maintained, older building located in the vicinity of Ned's office. The recently renovated architecture was ornate with intricate detailing around the windows and porte-cochere. For another trauma filled minute he sat without moving, forcing Elizabeth's pulse rate into the danger zone. She mentally listed the various elements of the structures looming just beyond the sidewalk and patches of grass, but every breath she drew was a struggle. Her heart pounded so hard she couldn't imagine MacBride not hearing it. Why didn't he say something?

Just when she thought she couldn't take anymore, he spoke. "You see that center window on the seventh floor?"

Elizabeth looked upward to the floor he'd indicated. She understood where they were and what he was trying to do. When her eyes focused on the center window, she answered, the hollow word a mere whisper, "Yes."

"That apartment belonged to Marissa Landon."

As Elizabeth stared at the dark window with its flower box overflowing with a bright spring mixture of blooms, the reality of what Annabelle had told her settled on her like a ton of bricks. Who would water those flowers now? Marissa was dead. Murdered.

"Do you know what arterial spray is?"

A hard knot formed in Elizabeth's stomach. "I don't want to hear this." The shaking that had plagued her in Annabelle's office started again.

"It's usually found near the victim of brutal violence," he went on cruelly. "The perpetrator has to inflict a wound that involves an artery. Like with Marissa. The slashing wound almost completely severed her head from her body. The carotid artery and the jugular were sliced clean through. Imagine the kind of evil it took to inflict that level of violence on another human being."

She squeezed her eyes shut and tried to block the gruesome images his words evoked. "Please, just take me back to my truck. I don't know anything."

Without a word he swerved away from the curb and merged into the traffic again. Her body was ice, her senses numb. She fought back the tears and silently screamed at the indignity, the senselessness.

How could she know anyone—have cared about someone—who would do something so heinous? Surely Brian couldn't be responsible for that kind of horror. But what if he was, and what if she did know something that would make a difference?

Could she live with herself if one more person died?

When MacBride parked once more, they were at Ned's office. Elizabeth blinked as confusion amplified the painful mixture of emotions twisting inside her.

"Why are we here?" Fear raced to the forefront of all else, and she turned to face MacBride. His blue eyes were dark with emotion. "Why did you bring me here?"

"Get out," he ordered. "We're going inside."

She reached for the door handle, but her hand shook so badly it took two attempts to open the door. Her head spun, making her movements awkward, unbalanced. What if MacBride had found the hidden door? What if he knew why she'd come here last night? She glanced quickly from side to side as he ushered her toward the front entrance. Had her being here last night somehow caused that brutal murder? Was Detective Brannigan waiting inside to interrogate her? Her chest ached with the floundering of her heart. She couldn't drag in a deep enough breath. She wanted it to stop—the murders, the suspicions, the fear. She just wanted it to stop.

MacBride used a key to open the front door, then locked it behind them once they were inside. Elizabeth sucked in a shallow breath and tried to calm herself. She couldn't let the panic take over now. She had to stay in control.

Sunlight filtered in through the half-closed blinds, dimly lighting the reception area. The air smelled stale already. The owner was dead, whatever kind of jerk he'd been. Whatever good he'd done in his life, if any, it was over. He was dead and so were four of his patients. Somehow she was a part of it.

She had to sit down. Elizabeth stumbled toward a chair and collapsed into it. "I don't want to be here," she murmured for all the good it would do. MacBride apparently wanted to punish her, to make her tell him what she knew, which was nothing that would matter. She was certain of it. If she'd thought for one second that anything she'd seen or heard or done would matter...

Except that one thing.

Mac wrestled back the sympathy that rose immediately as she crumpled beneath the weight of fear and guilt. He gritted his teeth, bracing for the charge that would accompany touching her, and took her by the arm to haul her to her feet "This way, Elizabeth."

She lurched forward, having little choice but to go with him or be dragged behind him. He took her into Harrison's private office, the one where he saw his patients, and herded her toward the leather chaise. He leaned against the edge of the massive desk and crossed his arms over his chest, cranking up the intimidation as he glared down at her.

She sat like a statue except for the fine tremor she couldn't hide. Before he could stop his traitorous eyes, he'd taken in every last detail of the way she looked today. She wore faded jeans and, unlike the overalls she usually donned for work, the jeans fit snugly, hugging her slender figure. The blouse was soft cotton, short-sleeved and buttoned up the front. One sneaker was about to come untied. But it was the way she wore her hair that unsettled him the most. It hung unrestrained over her shoulders. Her amber eyes stared up at him from behind those delicately rimmed glasses. She was scared to death, sick with dread at what she feared lay ahead.

By God, he intended to have some answers. Five people were dead. One might damn well have deserved a bad end, but the others were victims in the truest sense of the word. Whatever Elizabeth knew, whether she considered it relevant or not he would have it before they left this room.

"What do you want from me?" she asked, her voice unsteady.

"Is this where you spent all those hours with him?" The question was issued sharply, and Mac wanted to bite off his tongue when he recognized the emotion behind it. Jealousy. Damn it all to hell. He was jealous of a dead man's relationship with the woman who could very well be his killer. Except he didn't really believe that last part. He clenched his fists and fought the ridiculous feelings.

"Yes," she replied softly. Her fingers twisted together as she wrung her hands nervously. "Always right here," she volunteered to his surprise. "The first time I came he," her eyes took on a distant quality, "he insisted that comfort was of primary importance. I needed to relax and speak freely, knowing that anything I said or did in this office would never go any further."

Silence screamed for three beats as Mac realized how telling her final statement really was.

"But he lied to you, didn't he?"

She nodded. "His sessions were helpful at first. The panic attacks went away." She took a steadying breath and looked up at him. "Then he took our relationship to another level. He knew I needed more work to make it financially, so he offered to let me decorate his office. He was very kind to me." She blinked as if attempting to reason out the unreasonable. Her voice sounded machinelike, flat and emotionless. "That's when he…" She lapsed into silence, unable or unwilling to go on.

"He seduced you," Mac said from between gritted teeth.

She moved her head in what he took for a nod. "I didn't mean for it to happen. But he knew all the right things to say and…I needed to hear them." She stared at her clasped hands for a time. "It was a mistake. I should have seen through his machinations."

The blast of fury that roared through Mac forced him to his feet. Harrison had used her, just as he had all the others. But for Elizabeth it was different. The playing field hadn't been level—she was too naive to have any clue about the kind of world she'd allowed herself to be lured into. She wasn't like the others. Another jolt of anger shook him when he considered that he was falling for that same sad Cinderella story he'd predicted she would use to rationalize her actions.

He'd taken the bait hook, line, and sinker.

"So you killed him." He hurled the accusation at her, even though, at this point, he was reasonably sure she was innocent—of murder, anyway.

Her head came up and her face flushed. "No! How do I get that through to you, MacBride? I didn't kill him! We argued. I wished him…dead."

His name on her lips sent something like desire coursing through him, which only increased his fury. "But you know something about his death, don't you." He moved nearer to her, towered over her to achieve the effect he desired. It worked. She retreated as far as her position on the chaise would allow.

"I don't know." She shook her head, her brow lining in bewilderment. "I don't know who killed him."

"You went to his place that night, didn't you?" Mac outlined the scenario that had been forming in the back of his mind. Her startled gaze connected with his. "He stood you up and you were angry."

She looked away guiltily and he knew he'd hit the mark. "Did you have a fight? Is that how he got those scratches?"

She shook her head.

"Was he using the video for blackmail? Is that how he got to you?"

She bolted out of her seat, putting herself toe-to-toe with him. Anger glittered in her eyes. "Yes! Gloria and I found out about the videos and what he'd been up to with...with all of us." She blinked once, twice, clearly shocked she'd said so much.

"How did Gloria feel about that?" He'd already checked out Gloria's alibi. It was airtight. She'd been at dinner and the movies with her niece. It was always possible the niece was lying. "Did she want him dead, too?" What woman wouldn't after what Harrison had done to them?

"How do you think she felt?" Elizabeth spat. "But we didn't kill him," she countered, some of the bravado going out of her. "We were victims. Don't you get it?"

That was the trouble. He did get it. It took all his willpower to restrain the impulse to take her in his arms. He urged her back down onto the chaise, and then sat beside her. "Just tell me what happened, Elizabeth," he said gently. "That's all I want from you."

For a long time she simply sat there staring at her hands. Mac wished he knew the right words to say to somehow make her feel at ease. No words could make any of this right.

"I'd sworn I wouldn't ever speak to him again," she began wearily. "He'd hurt us too much. Almost cost Gloria and me our friendship. But he kept calling. He sounded so desperate. Finally he said he would give me the video if I'd have dinner with him one last time." She shrugged with the same weariness he heard in her voice. "I was desperate to get that video. We knew he had one on each of us. Gloria found out somehow."

Gloria Weston seemed to know a lot of things. He'd read Brannigan's report on his interview with her. Maybe Mac needed to question her himself. Brannigan had been thorough and he'd verified all statements. Funny thing was, now that he knew Gloria had been one of Ned's conquests, they hadn't found a video of her. Mac wondered how she'd managed to get hers from Harrison.

"Anyway, I went to the restaurant. Like a fool." Elizabeth laughed, a dry, humorless sound. "Of course he didn't show up." She shook her head. "I was so angry. I wanted to tell him just what I thought."

"So you went to his place." Mac had hoped that wasn't the case, but deep down he'd suspected as much. This was what had her running scared. She'd been so close to the murder without even knowing it.

She nodded. "I had to knock several times before he answered. When he did, it was obvious he'd been in bed with someone." She pressed her fist to her mouth as the tumultuous emotions shook her again. "I didn't think. I was furious. I just pushed past him and went straight to the bedroom. The sheets were tousled. The whole room smelled of sex. I screamed at him. I couldn't believe he'd kept me waiting while he had sex with someone else."

The idea that Harrison may have threatened her physically or even hurt her in some way tore at Mac's gut. Before he could prompt more answers, she went on.

"I demanded the video. He wouldn't give it to me." She exhaled a ragged breath, then chewed her lower lip for a moment. "We argued and he grabbed my arm and tried to make me listen to what he had to say."

Mac tensed as fresh rage gripped him.

"I fought him." She frowned. "I may have scratched him." She splayed her hands. "I don't know. It all happened so fast." A defeated sigh slipped past her lips. "He wouldn't give me the video, so I gave up. I warned him to stay away from me. Then I left."

His jaw ached from clenching it so tightly. "But no one saw you come or go?" He already knew the answer to that. Brannigan's men had questioned everyone in the building.

"I don't think so."

Mac scrubbed a hand over his face, the receding adrenaline leaving him weak." "Why didn't you tell me this in the beginning?"

"I was afraid you'd think I killed him."

Well, she'd been right to think that, although he'd considered her a prime suspect, anyway.

"You're sure no one else was there with Harrison when you left?"

She mulled over the question for a moment. "I'm pretty sure. I mean, I didn't go into the guest room or bathrooms." She closed her eyes, most likely retracing her movements in her mind. "I didn't go in the kitchen, either, but you can see beyond the island from the living room and I didn't notice anyone. I was pretty upset though."

Mac considered all she'd told him. There definitely could have been someone else there. "I still need that DNA sample from you. It's the only way I can prove you weren't in bed with him that night."

"Fine." She stiffened slightly. "I'll give you the sample."

Finally. Progress. "Tell me about last night."

Elizabeth had known that was coming. She'd made it through the initial part of her confession, but this part was going to be a little trickier. Her story would sound so farfetched. But what the hell? She had nothing to lose at this point and she was definitely out of options. Besides, MacBride wasn't going to give up until he had the truth. She had to respect that about him. He was trying to solve this case and maybe stop the murders. And if she could help, she wanted to.

"We had a kind of conference," she began.

"Who?" he interjected.

"Gloria, Annabelle and I."

"Annabelle Ford? Harrison's attorney?"

She stole a quick glance at him and almost shivered at the intensity in his eyes. And he was close. Closer than she'd realized. She resisted the urge to scoot away. Being afraid was over. She had to do this right. If anyone else died and it was in any way her fault for not telling all she knew...she couldn't live with that.

"Yes, Ned's attorney. Gloria called her when the third woman was murdered. We decided to see if we could put our heads together and figure out who was doing this."

MacBride sat perfectly still, his head inclined as he listened to her relate the details of her first meeting with Annabelle and Gloria. When she mentioned the Gentlemen's Association and the secret room, something changed in his eyes, but he masked it so quickly she wasn't sure exactly what she'd seen.

"I guess Brian was watching me," she suggested for lack of any other explanation. "We hadn't really seen each other except at an occasional party in months. I can't imagine how else he would have known. Even Annabelle and Gloria didn't know when I planned to make the attempt at getting in."

"Did he threaten you in any way?"

Elizabeth could feel the tension vibrating in the man sitting beside her. Something she'd told him had hit a nerve. She shook her head in response to his question. "Not at first. Then he started to make me feel uneasy. He tried to force me to admit I'd killed Ned." She quickly gave him the condensed version of the conversation. "It was like he thought he could make me say what he wanted to hear."

Mac couldn't stop himself. He had to touch her. He placed his hand atop her clasped ones. "Listen to me, Elizabeth. I can't elaborate much on the Gentlemen's Association, but I can tell you that the people involved with that group are not to be trusted or taken lightly. They're dangerous."

She looked up at him, her eyes wide with surprise behind her glasses. "Who are they?"

"That's what we're trying to find out. Did Novak say anything else about the Association? Something maybe you thought was insignificant?" Mac would damn well have Novak picked up this very hour. His mention of the Gentlemen's Association to Elizabeth was enough for probable cause.

After some consideration she shook her head. "No. That's all he said before I hit him."

He couldn't help the smile that broke loose at the idea of her crowning Novak. The self-serving bastard. "Okay. Shall we try and locate that secret room?"

She nodded jerkily and his protective instincts surged. Their eyes met and he knew in that instant she was without doubt completely innocent. He reached up to touch her face. He heard her breath catch, but she didn't draw away.

The ring of his cell phone shattered the moment.

It took a second ring for him to pull himself together enough to answer. "MacBride."

"Mac, it's Duncan."

He stood and moved away from the temptation she represented. "What's up?" The urge to loosen his tie had him reaching for his throat. The room was suddenly too damned hot.

"That guy, Novak."

"Yeah." The newest addition to Mac's I-wanna-pound-him list. "I was about to call you. I want you to—"

"His body was found in Central Park about an hour ago," Duncan interrupted.

The tangle of scenarios and possibilities fighting for attention in Mac's thoughts stopped dead. "You're sure it's him."

"Brannigan's partner ID'd him."

Mac let go a heavy breath. "I'm on my way."

"Wait" Duncan said before he could hang up. "You haven't heard the most bizarre part."

Mac braced himself for cause of death details. He always hated that part although those were the very details that gave an investigator the most information about the killer.

"The ME called your office this morning. It seems he found a match to the DNA evidence collected from the female victims in the Socialite case."

Mac was certain it had to be Novak. He wasn't sure how the ME had run across a DNA workup on Novak unless he'd been previously entered into CODIS under an alias.

"Remember all the DNA evidence that had to be checked out from Harrison's apartment?" Duncan asked.

"Get to the point." Mac was getting impatient here. He knew the drill.

"Well, the specimen in the first two victims was a match. The last two aren't completed yet, of course."

"A match to whom?" Mac snarled. Why the hell didn't he just spit it out?

"To Harrison," Duncan said "the DNA in both murders is a perfect match to Dr. Ned Harrison."

CHAPTER ELEVEN

Elizabeth stood numbly by as MacBride spoke to the caller. She was afraid to even imagine what had happened now. More bad news, she imagined. The tone of his voice left little doubt. Cold, flat.

She thought of her friend. MacBride had people watching Elizabeth, but what about Gloria? She needed protection, too. Annabelle had said there were at least four more names on the list the killer appeared to be using. Four more female patients she had reason to believe had carried on a personal relationship with Ned. Two of whom were Gloria and Elizabeth. Her nerves twisted a little tighter. What if another victim had been found?

MacBride ended the call. As he dropped his phone back into his pocket, she told herself she had no choice but to trust him. The suspicions Annabelle had offered were relevant to the case. Elizabeth had come clean with him about everything else that had happened last night and he'd listened. He'd covered her hand with his own, comforting her. She should tell him this part, too. Reading too much into his comforting gesture could be a mistake, but she couldn't restrain the urge. She was drawn to him, seriously drawn to him. Somehow the attraction went beyond the physical.

Right, Elizabeth. You're doing it again. Falling for the wrong guy. One who probably felt nothing for you except maybe sympathy.

But he felt something. Elizabeth had seen the hunger in his eyes. She saw the emotion in his eyes as he turned to face her now. There was a dread, not at seeing her, but at telling her the news he'd just received. Why would he care how it affected her if he didn't feel something for her? He'd rescued her from Brian even after she'd given his partner the slip. MacBride had likely sensed where she would go when the other man hadn't had a clue. He was tuned in to her on a very elemental level. Or maybe he'd simply had someone watching Ned's office as he'd claimed. Whatever the case, his arrival had been a good thing.

She felt reasonably sure that Brian would have come after her if he hadn't seen MacBride outside with her. Brian had clearly snapped out of the dazed state the whack on the head had sent him into and managed to slip away unseen. Tracking her down wouldn't have been a problem for him—except that MacBride had been watching over her. Like a guardian angel.

Slow down, Elizabeth. Even as she warned herself to take a step back, she felt the inevitable rush toward disaster.

MacBride moved toward her now, drawing her full attention back to the moment. Those intense blue eyes were guarded, which made her even more nervous. "Novak didn't mention talking to anyone else or expecting to meet with anyone else last night?"

A tendril of trepidation coiled inside her. They were back to Brian again. "No." Where was he going with this? "I don't know where he went afterward. He...he didn't call or anything." A burst of irritation chased away the trepidation. "If I'd heard from him, he would've gotten an earful." She was sick to death of being vulnerable—to MacBride or anyone else. Annabelle's theory nudged her again, shaking her newly found bravado.

"I'm not accusing you of anything, Elizabeth," Mac said more softly as he came nearer still. "There's been another development and we need to know if Novak mentioned meeting or speaking to anyone else."

Development? A chill raced over her. He meant another murder. "Who's dead?" Her voice gave away the fear building so fast she could hardly think much less breathe. "Just tell me, MacBride," she added with surprising strength.

He touched her. Placed his hand on her arm, nothing complicated or serious, just a touch. But the feelings the gesture engendered were entirely complicated.

"Novak is dead. His body was found in Central Park a little while ago."

Mac hadn't wanted to tell her like this, but she'd limited his options. She needed to know what was going on.

"How?" Her chin quivered ever so slightly and it was all he could do not to take her fully into his arms.

"I can't answer that for you just yet. Considering the speed with which these murders are occurring, I'd like to place you into protective custody for your own safety."

Fear, followed quickly by uncertainty, danced across her face. "I can't. I have to work."

"Elizabeth, it would be best—"

"Is someone watching Gloria, too?" she demanded.

Mac's worry began to manifest itself in an annoying ache behind his eyes. "Brannigan has one of his men keeping an eye on her, if that's what you're asking."

Her eyes glittered. "I want to know if someone is watching her every minute of the day and night."

He wondered if shock was setting in. She'd gone from wanting to know how Novak was murdered to whether or not Gloria Weston was being protected. The way she demanded a more precise response after he'd already given her an answer made him wonder if there was something more he should know. "Are you trying to tell me something, Elizabeth?"

A tremor went through her. "Annabelle has a theory. The murders," she cleared her throat of the emotion thickening there, "have occurred in alphabetical order. Adele, Bumbalough, Fowler, Landon. Annabelle believes there are four names left on the killer's list. Four more women who had an intimate relationship with Ned. Gloria and I are among those four. She thinks he won't stop until... we're all dead."

Mac had already suggested to Brannigan that the killer might be working in a nonrandom manner. Judging by the number of videos they'd found in Harrison's apartment, however, the number of potential victims was far greater than four.

"All the more reason for you to go into protective custody," he suggested, keeping the numbers to himself. The alphabetical theory had been shot down to an extent, anyway, when the Landon woman was found. The killer had skipped over at least three names between Fowler and Landon—names that went with videos they had discovered.

Elizabeth shook her head. "I have to finish this job." She looked directly at him, the urgency in her manner relaying just how important this was. "It can't wait. Boomer will be with me."

"Who needs protection with Boomer around?" Mac said dryly, regretting it the instant the words escaped.

"Look," Elizabeth said hotly, "I know you don't like him, but he's a good guy and I can depend on him."

Therein lay the crux of the matter, Mac realized. Elizabeth Young had been let down by too many people in her life. Her mother, her fiancé, her brother-in-law, even her father, who'd left her all alone when he died, and finally by her shrink. Trust didn't come easily to her. Being able to count on someone would mean a great deal to her. Even if it was an ex-con punk like Boomer.

"You're right," he admitted to her obvious surprise. "I want you to know that you can depend on me, as well. I'll see that someone is keeping an eye on Gloria."

She didn't bother to hide her amazement. "Thank you."

"I'm going to trust you with something, Elizabeth," Mac told her, only now making the decision to offer the information. "The Gentlemen's Association is why I'm here. These guys are nasty business. They're deep into Internet porn, mostly pretty young women like you, but some even younger. They have to be stopped. Harrison was my only bona fide connection. Novak was a close runner-up. Now they're both gone." He cranked up the intensity of his gaze, hoping to relay the utter desperation he felt. "I have to nail these guys, Elizabeth. I don't want anyone else hurt the way you were. I need evidence. Something. Anything to bring these guys down."

"The secret room," she said softly. "I know where it is."

Mac inspected the loft where Elizabeth and Boomer would be working today. He'd stationed Duncan in the corridor just outside the door and given him orders not to leave Elizabeth under any circumstances. Boomer, after a show of belligerence toward Mac's orders, had calmed down and told Mac in no uncertain terms that nothing would happen to Elizabeth while she was with him.

Mac didn't want to leave her. Dammit, he had a job to do, and still he didn't want to go. Apparently it had taken only one kiss to skew his judgment completely.

As he pointed his sedan in the direction of midtown, he forced his attention back to the case. The hidden room had proved to be the break he'd been hoping for. The room was completely sealed, shielded from any sort of detection. Harrison had covered every base. The room was totally self-sufficient and separate from the rest of his office. The power feed and telephone lines were split from a neighboring system, that of a legitimate business with nine-to-five operating hours. Never in a million years would that system have been checked. No one, not even Mac, would have thought of that one. The lines weren't connected to Ned Harrison in any way. Running lights and a few electronics wouldn't constitute enough of a draw to alert the other business that it was being systematically robbed.

This provided new insight into the way others in the Association were probably getting away with their sinister deeds without being caught.

An entire forensics team was at this very moment going through the room. The elaborate computer system would likely hold all the evidence they would need to lead them to others.

Mac should be back there himself, but first he had to see Brannigan. They needed to discuss this latest turn of events. There had to be a reasonable explanation for Harrison's DNA turning up at the crime scenes. Harrison was dead. Mac had viewed the body. He'd read the autopsy.

A theory churned in the back of his mind, but first he wanted to hear Brannigan's take.

Since the detective was still at the crime scene, Mac parked near the entrance to the walking zoo. Novak's body had been found next to a park bench where pigeons hung out hoping to be fed by the numerous daily visitors. He wondered if the location was significant. Maybe someone thought Novak had talked.

Five minutes later Mac stood next to Brannigan as the ME's office took away the body. The autopsy would be needed for confirmation, though it appeared Novak had been bludgeoned to death. The irony that Elizabeth had hit him on or near the temple wasn't lost on Mac. According to the ME, time of death was possibly within mere hours of that of Marissa Landon. The location wasn't that far from the Landon apartment.

"No signs of struggle," Brannigan said, then added dryly, "other than the pulp his head was beaten into."

"You think someone just sneaked up on him out here in the dark?" Mac queried, not certain he agreed with that theory.

"His wallet is missing," Brannigan said. "But it seems a little overkill for a simple robbery."

Mac made an agreeable sound. "Whoever did this wanted to ensure he didn't survive."

"Well, that takes Novak off the suspect list." Brannigan puffed out a weary breath. "I thought for sure he might be our man. Especially after he disappeared on us last night. It seems every time a murder has occurred, he managed to be AWOL."

"What about the DNA connection to Harrison?" Mac asked, getting to the heart of the matter. "How's forensics explaining that little quandary?"

"They're checking to see if it had been refrigerated or frozen prior to finding its way inside our vics." The older man shrugged, the movement calling attention to the poor fit of his jacket "Maybe Harrison had been storing up for a rainy day and somebody decided to use his stash to throw us off."

Mac rubbed his chin, absently noting that he needed a shave. "We need to check into the brother," he suggested. "We know Harrison is dead, there's no question. And yes, someone could be planting the evidence. It isn't impossible, but neither is the concept that the brother isn't dead. We haven't seen his body for confirmation. Who's to say the guy isn't alive and well and seeking his vengeance for his brother's death? We both believe that Harrison was killed by a woman. What if the brother believes it as well? He can't be sure which of the former lovers is guilty, so he takes them out one at a time, knowing eventually he'll get the right one."

"Nigel Harrison died four years ago," Brannigan countered. "He's buried in some hell hole down in Mexico. How the devil am I supposed to verify that he's really dead? We damn sure can't rely on any paperwork they send us. And if he's alive, where has he been all this time? No one I've interviewed even knew Dr. Harrison had a brother."

"I want him exhumed," Mac said grimly, fury pumping through him. "We've got four murder victims with Harrison's DNA swimming around inside them." The idea that Elizabeth could be next screamed at him. He clenched his jaw until he regained some semblance of self-control. When he'd investigated Harrison's background months ago, he'd learned about the brother, but that detail hadn't mattered—the brother was dead. But now they had reason to believe otherwise. Especially considering this latest turn of events.

"The brother's an identical twin—he could have the same DNA structure. I want to know if the bastard is really dead or if he's alive and avenging his brother's death."

"So we're going ghost hunting now?" Brannigan mused, only half joking.

"Maybe," Mac allowed, "but it would be a mistake to overlook that avenue just because we *think* it isn't viable. I want to *know.*"

Brannigan shoved his hands into his trousers and ducked his head between his shoulders. "Your people can get an order like that faster than I can.

You know the chain of command I'm forced to work with."

Mac reached for his cell. "I'll take care of it" He hesitated before entering the necessary number. "If you're not keeping Gloria Weston under surveillance twenty-four/seven, I think you should. Annabelle Ford, too."

"We've got someone watching the Weston woman. You think the mouthpiece needs surveillance, too?"

"She seems to know an awful lot about Harrison's extracurricular activities." Mac tried to pinpoint his reservations where Annabelle Ford was concerned, but couldn't. "There's something about her that nags at me."

Brannigan scoffed. "She's a freakin' lawyer, enough said."

"Push the ME for DNA analysis on Novak, too," Mac added as an afterthought "He's about the same size as Harrison was. A little more muscular, but the height is right. He could be the brother. Who knows? With the cosmetic-surgery possibilities out there today; it could be anyone with a similar build."

Brannigan gave him a two-fingered salute and then strode in the direction of the ME's van where Novak's body was now safely ensconced. Mac stared at his cell phone for a second and considered that it would take some powerful influence to get this exhumation under way ASAP. He had a friend or two in D.C., so he might as well start there.

Why bother with the bottom when he could start at the top?

Elizabeth paced the room again, stopping every few minutes to peek out the window. Agent Duncan was still there, watching her apartment. It was past seven and she was exhausted. She and Boomer had worked until six and had made a good deal of progress. By then she'd been so wired up thinking about all that had happened she'd had to call it a day. Boomer had offered to come stay with her, but with Duncan right outside she didn't see the point. Besides, he probably had a date. Boomer always had a date.

She'd called Gloria to make sure she was at her sister's. Elizabeth couldn't help feeling hurt all over again as Brian's words echoed through her. He had to have been lying. She refused to believe that Gloria would do that to her. Elizabeth closed her eyes and collapsed on the sofa. No matter that she'd firmly decided to put that behind her, it pushed to the forefront yet again.

Brian was dead.

He'd been a jerk who hurt her and still she couldn't help feeling bad that he was dead. No one deserved to die a violent death like that. She shuddered when she considered the last two men with whom she'd been involved had come to tragic ends. Then again, she doubted it had anything to do with her. Both had been deeply involved in very dangerous hobbies. A finger of dread slid down her spine when she thought of all she'd seen in that hidden room this morning.

Dozens of pictures of women, some far younger than her, in degrading poses. How could she not have recognized how utterly sick Ned was? And if Brian were—had been, she amended with another quake of dread—involved with that kind of thing, he was pretty damned sick, too. Where was her intuition on the subject of men? It seemed she was utterly blind when it came to the opposite sex. Her naiveté had gotten her into real trouble this time.

Did the members of the Gentlemen's Association see women as nothing more than pieces of meat? Or as mere play things?

The idea that she had been a part of that, even unknowingly, made her ill. She wanted—needed— to be able to depend on Mac. She rolled her eyes. There she went, calling him Mac again. She wrung her hands and tried to reason out the issue. What if she trusted him and he let her down the way every- one else had? She closed her eyes and confessed that truth. She needed him. She wasn't sure she could get through this alone, and her relationship with Gloria was off somehow right now. At the same time that thought went through her mind, she told her- self it was foolish. She could trust Gloria. Brian had lied. That was all.

A knock at her door startled her from the trou- bling thoughts. She stood, propelled as much by fear as by the instinct to answer the door. She peeked out the window. Her heart almost stopped. Duncan's

car was gone. Frantically she scanned the area surrounding the house. With immense relief she noted
Mac's sedan in the driveway.

Letting go the breath she'd been holding, she
hurried to the door. As she reached for the lock she
remembered what he'd told her. "Who is it?"

"It's me," his deep voice resonated through the
wooden slab between them.

Something warmer than relief washed over her,
and she quickly unlocked and opened the door.
"Nothing else has happened, has it?" She was suddenly afraid he'd come here to give her more bad
news. She'd just spoken to Gloria. She was safe for
now.

He shook his head. "Nothing new. I just wanted
you to know that I'd be out there watching tonight."

She nodded mutely. He looked exhausted. She
wondered why he didn't just assign another of his
men to take over.

"Call me if you need me."

When he would have headed back down the
stairs, she abruptly regained her voice. "Could you
come in for a while?" He stopped but didn't turn.
She snapped her mouth shut and called herself
every kind of idiot. What was she doing?

Slowly, as if considering the prudence of that
offer, as well, he turned to face her. Those blue eyes
directed that very question at her.

She attempted a nonchalant shrug but managed
only a stiff jerk of one shoulder. "I just thought we
could talk for a while." She folded her arms to hide

the way her hands had begun to shake. "I guess I'm a little rattled." She heaved a mighty breath. "Or restless."

"For a few minutes," he relented, moving deliberately toward her. When he stood in the doorway staring down at her, he qualified, "I'll leave it up to you to let me know when it's time to go."

She nodded and stepped back so he could come inside. When she'd locked the door, she turned to find him standing in the middle of the room watching her. She summoned a smile. "Would you like coffee or tea?"

He shook his head, his gaze focused heavily on her.

She told herself she was simply tired. It had been a long day. Hell, it had been a long week. The faces of all those women floated briefly before her eyes. The realization that Ned and Brian were dead. Murdered. And then the undeniable fact that she could be next. She swayed.

Mac was at her side in a flash. "You should sit down."

Elizabeth leaned on him as he walked her to the sofa. "Thanks," she mumbled as he released her.

"Maybe you're the one who needs some tea," he suggested.

For a moment she relished the feeling of having someone worry about her. Then she shook her head and chastised herself for behaving so foolishly. "Please, just keep me company for a while."

He dropped into the ancient overstuffed chair directly across from her and appeared content to simply watch her.

She looked away, suddenly at a loss as to what they should talk about. Here she'd practically begged him to stay and now she'd apparently turned mute. Well, she might not be able to initiate a conversation, but her blood was rapidly reaching the boiling point. He'd shed his jacket and tie. She couldn't recall ever seeing him without his tie. A couple of buttons were loosened. Longing sent her pulse into a faster rhythm. What was wrong with her?

Her gaze bumped his and for several beats she couldn't look away. Naked hunger flashed fleetingly in his eyes. That awareness sent renewed need swirling through her. She wasn't the only one having trouble with the building tension. She felt a smile tickle her lips at the idea that he wanted her. It seemed so...so unlikely, and yet she'd known from the very beginning that something sizzled between them.

With effort she directed her gaze elsewhere. To the faded rug, then the tattered fabric of the sofa.

"You checked in with your friend Gloria?"

Her head came up. Was it her imagination, or was his voice strained? She blinked and searched his face for any hint of that sexual hunger she'd thought she saw moments ago. Evidently he'd banished it or she'd imagined it.

"She's fine."

He nodded once. "Good."

The seconds turned into minutes as the silence thickened around them again. What had she been thinking? She should have known this wouldn't work. She just wasn't the type to play the part of seductress and he obviously wasn't that interested or he would make a move.

She closed her eyes in self-disgust. What was wrong with her? People were dying all around them. How could she be thinking about sex?

"Well." Mac stood. "I'll be outside if you need me."

Her eyes popped open and she scrambled to her feet "Um...okay." She didn't want him to go. Dammit. She'd never been good at this. Somehow she'd always made the wrong choices or simply been too afraid to go after what she really wanted. For once in her life she wanted to take charge and go for it. She wanted *him.*

Mac paused at the door. "Good night."

Refusing to hesitate long enough to think, she grabbed him by his shirtfront and pulled his mouth down to hers. She closed her eyes tightly and she kissed him. For one terrifying moment all she could think was that this wouldn't work. He resisted. Didn't take her in his arms. Didn't kiss her back. Defeat tugged at her fledgling determination. She couldn't do this. Then the marvelous textures of his lips and mouth penetrated her senses fully and she got lost in the feel and taste of him. He kissed her back, and then he took charge of the kiss.

He devoured her with his mouth, his jaw scratchy and rough but more tantalizing than any sensation she'd ever known. His fingers plunged into her hair as he deepened the kiss. She could feel the fierce energy radiating just beneath the surface of his hot skin. Those skilled hands slid down her back and suddenly he was touching her everywhere at once, stripping off her clothes, baring her skin to his greedy hands and mouth. His fingers set her on fire every place he touched. She was losing control and she wanted him to lose control with her.

She tugged at the buttons of his shirt until her hands flattened fully against the muscled terrain beneath. The heat of his skin seared her palms. She moaned and somehow his mouth found hers again. His kiss was insanely sexy. He pulled her body hard against his and carried her to the bedroom, all the while his mouth plundered hers. He tasted hot and strong, like dark, fragrant coffee. She wanted him to awaken every part of her body. To turn her into the kind of woman who could bring a man like him to his knees.

She wanted to see his vulnerable side, to find his weakness if it took all night long. She wanted to forget everything, to make the world go away for just this one night.

They stripped off the last of the restrictive garments, touching, teasing each new expanse of skin they uncovered. He felt so incredibly hot and hard. His muscles were beautifully defined, his body perfectly proportioned. She wanted to learn all of him, wanted to taste the sweet and the salty. Broad, broad shoulders and a sculpted chest narrowed into a lean waist and hips. Incredibly strong arms that lifted her nude body against that tempting torso and lowered her to the bed. Long, muscular legs and strong, confident hands. He came down over her and she smiled as she considered the other generous part of him. His thick sex nudged between her thighs, and for the first time in her life she opened freely, without undue coaxing.

She wanted this. She wanted him. She stared into the fiery blaze of those dark-blue eyes and knew this was going to be special. Whatever repercussions tomorrow brought, this moment was worth it.

She gasped when his body drew away from hers, but she soon discovered that he had other plans. He trailed hot, wet kisses along her flesh until he reached his ultimate destination. With the first flick of his tongue she melted into a tangle of shivery sensations. Moan after moan drifted from her lips as he positioned her for full access and lapped hungrily at her sensitized flesh. He pushed her closer and closer to the brink until she was writhing and pleading for him to finish it. She felt ready to combust with the mounting pleasure.

She screamed his name and somehow his mouth came down on hers as he simultaneously drove into her. He thrust fully, deeply and for the first time she was utterly primed, slick and yielding. Muscles that had once resisted this very moment opened eagerly to him, welcomed the marvelous friction of his rigid male body along her skin and thrusting deep, deep inside her. He cupped her face in his hands and kissed her tenderly, his hips setting the perfect rhythm, not too fast, not too slow. The world narrowed until there was nothing but his weight, his breath, his strong hands, and the plunge and slide of him.

The new spiral of pleasure started so, so far away and then suddenly she was caught up in a hurricane. He brought her all the way to completion, making her forget everything but him and his touch.

CHAPTER TWELVE

Mac lay in Elizabeth's bed as the sun rose the next morning. They'd made love over and over again during the night. She'd come alive in his arms just as he'd longed for her to do. His gut clenched when he thought of how she could tear him apart with that luscious mouth.

She lay in his arms now, sleeping peacefully, trustingly. Her glasses were on the bedside table and their clothes were spread all over the apartment. His pulse began to race as he inventoried the way her body was wrapped around his. One creamy thigh was draped across his hip. Her arms were curled around his neck. Her sweet face was nestled against his chest. And those lovely breasts were flattened against him. Her long hair splayed over his flesh like raw silk. There wasn't a part of him that didn't ache for her even after hours of mind-blowing sex.

No coddling or coaxing had been necessary. She'd kissed him first and she hadn't slowed down until she'd fallen asleep, exhausted and sated. She'd explored his body without hesitation. After her second climax she'd rolled him over and climbed atop to ride to completion once more. Her appetite and eagerness had matched his in every way. She'd licked and sucked and kissed him until he'd thought he would lose his mind or simply die.

And she was his.

His arms tightened around her.

Whether Elizabeth Young realized it yet or not, he never intended to let her go.

"What time is it?" she murmured sleepily, those tempting lips moving against his skin.

"Time for both of us to get to work." Mac knew she kept long hours just as he did. On the job early and didn't stop until it was done. That was something they had in common, loyalty and determination. He respected those traits in her. He also respected her ability to make him hard with scarcely a touch even after a night like last night.

"Hmm...I see we're *up* already," she teased.

He rolled her onto her back and smiled down at her. God, he loved how she looked first thing in the morning. All soft and pretty and relaxed. "Honey," he growled, "up will never be the problem as long as I'm within three feet of you."

They made love again and then they showered together. Mac swore as he wrapped a towel around her damp body that he would not let this moment end. He would not let her down.

No one would ever hurt her again.

Elizabeth couldn't remember ever being this happy. Not even when she thought she had the world by the tail after Brian's proposition that she come away with him. A flash of regret stung her at the memory that he was dead, but she forced it away. She'd cared for him, was sorry that he was dead, but never in her life had she felt the way she did at this moment about any man.

She studied Mac's profile as he parked in front of the building where Boomer was already at work. Mac had insisted on seeing her to work, and Duncan would take over from there for a few hours. After all, Mac had a case to solve. A warm glow started deep inside her at the idea of how protective he was of her. She'd never known that feeling of security with anyone except her father.

This was good. She knew it with complete certainty.

She smiled.

This was very good.

She didn't want it to end. Ever.

Mac switched off the engine and turned to her, propping his arm on the back of the seat. "I've debated whether I should tell you this or not, but I feel like I have to."

Fear trickled into her veins. "What?" She didn't want to hear anything bad. She wanted desperately to hang on to this happy moment.

"The killer left behind some evidence at each scene. DNA analysis is back on the first two victims."

She nodded, not sure exactly what that meant.

"All the victims were sexually assaulted."

"Do you think it was Brian?" Could he have been that kind of monster? How could she have been so blind?

Mac hesitated before answering, and in that moment her instincts warned that it was far worse than she expected.

"The DNA was a perfect match to Harrison's."

Shock plowed through her. For a moment she couldn't breathe. "But he's dead," was all she could say.

Mac nodded. "Yes, he is. That's confirmed." He searched her face and she knew the pain on his was related to the anxiety he saw on hers. "Did you know he had an identical twin brother?"

That news startled her all over again. "No. I mean yes. Annabelle told us he had a brother who'd died, but she didn't mention he was a twin."

"They grew up bouncing around in foster care. Both managed to turn a bad beginning into bright futures." Mac tapped the steering wheel as if contemplating how much more he should tell her. "His brother reportedly died four years ago."

"If he's dead and Ned is…"

Mac leveled his gaze on hers. "Ned Harrison is dead," he confirmed. "But, we haven't confirmed the brother's death. We're working on it. I just wanted you to know that someone out there might be out for vengeance. If he thinks you or one of the other women killed his brother, that may be what we're dealing with here."

Icicles formed in her chest. "So I should be on the lookout for a carbon copy of Ned." This was too much. One Ned Harrison was more than enough.

"Not necessarily," Mac countered. "He may have altered his appearance, surgically and otherwise. If he faked his death, there's likely a reason and being recognized would not be a part of his plan, I suspect."

She exhaled an exasperated breath. "So basically he could be anyone."

Mac nodded. "Basically. *If* he's alive."

His fingers trailed along her hairline, sending a delicious stir of sensations through her as he tucked a stray tendril behind her ear. It didn't pay to braid one's hair while being kissed by a man like Collin MacBride. She probably had dozens of wisps hanging about.

"Don't take any chances, Elizabeth. Stay close to Boomer. Don't wander out of Duncan's watch. I need you to be careful." He shook his head and looked away for a moment. "To be honest with you, I'm tempted to arrest you and force you to go into protective custody—"

"You promised," she interrupted. "I have to work. Finishing this project is too important. It can make or break me."

"I know. I won't break that promise." His gaze found hers once more. "But I need you to swear to me you won't take any chances. We can't be sure who we're looking for here. It could be someone from the Gentlemen's Association who had a thing for Harrison or who wanted him shut down. The DNA evidence may have been planted."

"I won't take any chances, I swear."

Still not happy about her decision, Mac walked her to the door of the loft. Boomer promised not to allow her out of his sight. Duncan took up watch right outside the door.

Elizabeth was pretty sure she wouldn't soon forget Mac's goodbye kiss. If the desperation behind it was any indication, he was as deep in this as she was.

And she was in way over her head.

Around lunchtime loud voices erupted in the corridor outside the loft. Boomer and Elizabeth exchanged questioning looks before she recognized the voice railing at Duncan.

Annabelle.

Elizabeth put her paint roller aside and rushed into the corridor to intervene. In one glance she summed up the situation. Duncan was hell bent on doing his job of protecting Elizabeth, and Annabelle was equally determined to see her.

"It's okay, Agent Duncan," Elizabeth said quickly. "Annabelle's a friend."

Giving the resigned man a triumphant glare, Annabelle stormed past him and into the loft with Elizabeth.

"We have to talk," she whispered from the corner of her mouth. Her gaze flicked to Boomer on the other side of the loft.

"Sure." Nerves jangling, Elizabeth ushered her toward the one area that was separated from the main part of the loft—the bathroom.

Once within the confines of the smaller room, Annabelle blurted her statement in what was probably an attempt at whispering. "Brian Novak is dead."

Elizabeth nodded solemnly. "I know."

Annabelle took her hands in hers. "I'm so sorry, Elizabeth. I had to be sure you were all right. I know how close the two of you once were." She glanced toward the open door. "I don't want you to worry, dear. I didn't tell them anything about the other night."

A frown of confusion worked its way across Elizabeth's brow. "You didn't tell who?"

Annabelle rolled her gray eyes in impatience. "That brutish Detective Brannigan. He spoke to me and to Gloria. She called, extremely upset. I rushed over here immediately, since you weren't answering your cell."

Dammit. She'd totally forgotten her phone. Mac had consumed her thoughts. "I appreciate that you wanted to protect me, but you didn't have to worry or hide anything about the other night in Ned's office."

Annabelle squeezed, her hands knowingly. "Oh, but you're wrong. That ridiculous detective thinks you killed Brian. He thinks you killed Ned, too!"

A little jolt of shock rumbled through Elizabeth. "Are you sure?"

The older woman huffed in exasperation. "Why, the imbecile said as much. He was rambling on about how the FBI had been watching you from the beginning and how they'd taken the case away from him." She released Elizabeth so she could throw up her hands. "He was furious with MacBride for horning in on his prime suspect. MacBride told Brannigan he couldn't handle you so he was taking over."

"When did MacBride say all this?" The detectives assertions didn't make sense. Mac wanted to protect her. Brannigan was wrong. He had to be.

"Talk to Gloria," Annabelle urged. "She came away from the meeting with the same feeling. You've got to call that criminal lawyer you put on retainer before you find yourself appearing before a grand jury."

"I will." Elizabeth's words were thin. It took all the strength she could rally to hold back the misery mushrooming inside her. "I'll call him today."

Apparently satisfied with that assurance, Annabelle warned her again to be careful, and then rushed away. Agent Duncan looked none too happy about the visit. Elizabeth didn't care. Right now the only thing she cared about was confirming the worst.

If Mac was using her to close his case...she squeezed her eyes shut and fought the tears. She couldn't believe he would do that. Mac had protected her. Made love to her as no one else had. She'd opened up to him, been the wanton woman she'd secretly longed to be with the right man. It couldn't have been a lie.

She wouldn't let it be.

Annabelle was upset. She'd probably taken it all out of context. Elizabeth knew from experience that Brannigan could be a brash SOB. He could be trying to make Mac look bad.

She would not lose trust in Mac—not without solid proof, anyway.

Elizabeth got another hour of hard work behind her before she lost the war with her emotions. She couldn't ignore what she had to do any longer. She gave Boomer instructions for the rest of the day. Not that he really needed any. He worked well on his own.

Now came the hard part. She exited the loft and found Duncan propped on the window ledge at the end of the corridor, sipping coffee from a thermos. The window's view wasn't anything to write home about, just the uncommonly wide alleyway between this old industrial building and the next. At least it allowed sunlight into the otherwise dark corridor.

"I need to go to Gloria Weston's office."

Duncan stood abruptly. "I'm not sure that's such a good idea. We'll have to check with Mac before going anywhere."

Elizabeth wasn't about to be thwarted. "You can either take me now or I'll use Boomer's van."

"Let me give Mac a quick call." Duncan withdrew his cell and entered the number. After thirty seconds or so it was obvious he wasn't going to reach Mac. "He must be on another call."

"I'd like to go now, please," she informed him, leaving no room for argument. She was going to Gloria's office one way or another. Something wasn't right. She kept replaying the conversation she'd had with Annabelle and something felt off.

Duncan finally relented. "All right. I guess it won't hurt."

Half an hour later they were on the elevator headed toward the eighteenth floor and Gloria's office. Duncan fit right in with all the suits and ties. Elizabeth, however, stood out like a sore thumb. Her jeans and t-shirt, both dappled with white paint looked vastly out of place.

"You can wait here," she said to Duncan when they reached Gloria's door.

"I'll need to check it out first."

Blowing out a puff of frustration, Elizabeth stood back and allowed him to knock and then enter Gloria's office.

"Miss Young would like to see you." She heard him say. Wow, finally, she had her own secretary, as well as bodyguard. All it had taken was a few unsolved murders.

He stepped back into the corridor as Gloria peeked out from her office, her eyes wide with surprise. "What's going on?"

Elizabeth thanked Duncan before following Gloria into her office and closing the door behind them. "You know Brian is dead."

Gloria nodded grimly. "I can't believe it. Do you know they think he's the one who's been killing all the women?"

Elizabeth didn't remember Annabelle saying that. "They do?"

"It's hard to believe, I know. But that's the impression Detective Brannigan gave me."

"He said he thought Brian was the killer?" Elizabeth pressed. She had to know how this was going down. Had to understand her position in all this.

Gloria frowned thoughtfully for a moment. "No, he didn't exactly say it. I just got those vibes from him and the slant of his questions."

"Did he say anything about me?" Elizabeth held her breath, not sure she could cope with the answer if it matched what Annabelle had said.

Gloria flipped her hands palms up in a noncommittal gesture. "He did mention you." She dropped onto the edge of her desk. "It was odd. He didn't exactly accuse you of anything, but I got the impression he somehow thought you and Brian were in on this together." She pulled a cocky face. "But I set him straight on that one. You and Brian hadn't been in on anything together in months."

Her words warmed Elizabeth. "Thanks." She moistened her lips, then gnawed on her lower one for a second. "Annabelle came by. She was extremely upset. She said Brannigan considered me the prime suspect in Ned's as well as Brian's murder. She said he'd gotten the impression the FBI thought so, as well. She…" Elizabeth shrugged. "I don't know. The more I think about it, the weirder the conversation seems."

Frowning, Gloria shook her head slowly. "He didn't say anything like that to me, but he did ask a lot of questions about you and Ned and you and Brian." Her frown deepened. "Now that you mention it, he did lean heavily toward tying you to both men. He kept bringing up your name each time he talked about Ned or Brian's murder."

That too-familiar chill crept into Elizabeth's bones. "But he didn't mention the FBI's thoughts on the matter?"

"No. I'm sure he didn't." Gloria shrugged. "Then again, I made it clear that you and I are friends. Maybe he held back, knowing I'd likely tell you whatever he said."

That was true. Since there was no reason for him to suspect Elizabeth and Annabelle had any sort of relationship, he would likely speak more freely around her. Anxiety coiled in her stomach once more.

"Don't sweat Annabelle. I've gotten the occasional creepy vibe from her, too. She is a lawyer, after all." Gloria rubbed her forehead with her thumb and forefinger. "I just wish this were over."

"Me, too." Elizabeth leaned against the corner of the desk next to her friend. "There's something I have to ask you, Gloria."

Her friend turned to look at her, her gaze expectant. "You know you can ask me anything."

Elizabeth had sworn to herself she wouldn't visit this place, but she needed all of it over and done with. No secrets. No lingering questions. "When Brian confronted me at Ned's office, he said some hurtful things."

Gloria harrumphed. "Well, I hate to speak ill of the dead, but there's no surprise there."

Elizabeth moistened her lips and worked up the nerve to say the rest. "He said you recommended me to Ned after *he* told you to. That you were in on the whole thing. His using me and then Ned doing the same."

Gloria's expression had gone from calm and patient to outraged in less than three seconds. "You're kidding, right?"

Elizabeth gave her head a little shake. "I didn't believe him, but I wanted you to know—"

"What do you mean, you didn't believe him?" Gloria demanded, her tone filled with hurt. "You're asking me, so you must have believed it to some degree." She threw up her hands and pushed away from her desk. "I can't believe you would even con- sider his lies as having any merit whatsoever."

Duncan stuck his head inside the door. "Everything all right in here?"

The two severe glowers thrown his way sent him ducking back into the corridor.

"Gloria," Elizabeth urged, "I didn't believe him. I—"

"You didn't?" Her friend was angry now. A flush had turned her pale skin a deep crimson. "Well, you could have fooled me. Why would you bother bringing it up if you didn't?"

She was right. Elizabeth stared at the floor, ashamed of herself for believing Brian even for a second. "I'm sorry. I don't know—"

"I do," Gloria snapped, her arms folded over her chest in an unyielding manner. "You have that little faith in our friendship." Mouth set in a grim line, she skirted the desk and began to shuffle through the mound of papers lying there. "If you'll excuse me, I have work to do."

"Let's not leave it like this, please," Elizabeth pleaded. "I was wrong to let him get to me, but I—"

Gloria held up a hand. "I can't talk about this right now, I'm too upset. Please, just go."

Elizabeth moved to the door, but hesitated before going through it. "Just remember one thing," she said softly. Gloria didn't bother looking up. "This isn't your fault. It's mine. I'm the one with the trust issues. I jumped the gun here and I'm sorry. No matter what happens with all this insanity, you're still my best friend."

Elizabeth didn't wait for a reply. Gloria was too hurt right now. But they would work it out... somehow.

She sat numbly in Duncan's car as he headed back toward SoHo. His cell rang and she jerked at the sound. Swiping the infuriating tears from her cheeks, she forced a deep breath and kept her gaze straight ahead. She tried not to think, but it was impossible. The events of the past two weeks were spinning in her head, crashing down on her with a sense of finality that threatened her tenuous grip on composure. Ned's deceit. His murder. The police. The murdered women. Brian's preposterous accusations. His murder. Making love with Mac.

God, please let her be able to trust him. To count on that one thing. She couldn't live with another letdown.

"It's Mac," Duncan said. "He needs to talk to you."

Her hand shaking, Elizabeth took the phone. "Hello." She cringed at the quaver in her voice. Strong. She had to be strong.

"Elizabeth, listen to me." The sound of his voice was reassuring. "There's been another murder. I've instructed Agent Duncan to take you home and to stay with you until I can get back there."

She listened, too stunned to reply. Some part of her brain niggled at her, reminding her that she really needed to work, but she couldn't quite grasp the initiative.

"Brannigan is sending another man over to keep watch on Gloria."

Her friend's name startled her out of her trance. "Annabelle said there's still one more before he gets to Gloria and me." God, she prayed her information was correct. What was she thinking? She was wishing the danger on someone else, someone just as innocent as they were. "Whoever she is, she'll need protecting, too."

Silence roared between them for a moment that felt like an eternity. Why didn't he say something?

"If Harrison had another female patient whose name comes alphabetically after the latest victim and before Weston, I can't find it in his files."

Fear broadsided Elizabeth.

If Mac was right, Gloria was next.

CHAPTER THIRTEEN

Elizabeth retraced her steps across her suddenly too-small living room. She'd never noticed before that the old wooden floor creaked in a certain spot about three feet from the rear wall. It squeaked smack-dab in the center, too. She'd never really had time to pace the floor that much or to be aware it made any sounds. Or maybe she'd simply been too exhausted by the time she dragged herself home at night. Whenever her panic attacks had struck at home, she'd done her walking off of the excess adrenaline outside. It worked better that way. Now that she thought about it, this apartment had really served as nothing more than the place to sleep and shower. It hadn't really been a home.

Her life had been in too much of an uproar and she'd been far too busy attempting to make ends meet to worry about anything else. The worn area rug and meager furnishings had been included with the place, for which she'd been immensely grateful. She'd had nothing of her own.

Nothing but a boxful of mementoes from the life she'd once lived in a small Maryland town. It felt like a dozen lifetimes ago now.

She hadn't even bothered calling her sister, the only family she had left, and telling her about the murders or her connection to any of it. Her only sibling had enough troubles of her own. Fortunately for the kids, Peg had straightened out her life since becoming a widow. No more drugs or drinking. She even had a job. While working at the local Walmart might not sound like much to most, it was a huge step for Peg. Elizabeth's little sister had never been much for responsibility, and she hadn't really grown up until her third child was born.

Elizabeth couldn't blame all the trouble on her sister. With a mother who deserted them and a father who'd been too busy working to keep a roof over their heads to influence their raising to any degree, what else could one expect?

She was rambling down memory lane, as fruitless as it was, to avoid facing reality.

In the past a situation this stressful would have thrown her into full-scale panic, but strangely she felt a sense of calm. Her concern for her friend had overridden all else. Elizabeth turned and started across the room, once more silently willing the telephone to ring. She needed to hear from Gloria. She'd called her office as soon as she arrived home, but her assistant had informed her that Gloria had gone for the day. She'd called Gloria's cell a dozen times and gotten no answer. Then she'd called Gloria's sister's house, and there hadn't been any answer there either.

Uneasiness ate away at Elizabeth, but she stayed strong. She should have heard from Mac by now.

What was going on with the latest victim? Had he gotten in touch with Brannigan about Gloria?

Elizabeth deviated from her usual route and pushed the curtain aside just far enough to see Duncan's car outside. She didn't see him in the fading daylight, but she knew he was around, watching the yard and alley, checking the doors and windows. She'd offered him some coffee, but he'd declined, saying that his wife always made him a thermos full each morning. Elizabeth wondered vaguely what it would be like to have that kind of relationship. Taking care of each other's needs, always knowing someone to depend on was there. She closed her eyes and thought about making love with Mac. Long nights, cradled in his arms, sated emotionally, as well as physically.

Never count your chickens before they hatch, darling, her daddy had always said. She, of all people, should know that adage was true. She knew better than to start thinking about forever where Mac was concerned. They'd shared one night, nothing more. When this case was over, assuming she survived it, they would probably never see each other again. He could have a girlfriend…or a fiancée.

The bottom fell out of her stomach. They really hadn't talked that much. What did she actually know about him? He'd been born and raised in Washington, D.C. Had a degree from Columbia. He was thirty-five and he'd been with the FBI for ten years. She had no idea if he had any family or even what foods he liked or what his favorite color was.

The panic she'd been certain wouldn't strike suddenly did. It tightened her throat, made her skin crawl, as her heart kicked into overdrive and unneeded adrenaline rocketed through her veins.

"Walk it off," she muttered, disgusted with her inability to control the reaction. Damn, she hated being vulnerable to her own traitorous body.

She grabbed the phone and punched in the number for Gloria's sister's house. When she got no answer she tried her friend's cell again.

Still no answer.

Still no word from Mac.

She couldn't take it anymore.

She punched in another number and the answer came after the first ring. "Speak."

Despite the pressure building inside her, she almost laughed at Boomer's barked greeting. "Boomer, I need your help."

Forty-five minutes later Elizabeth climbed into Boomer's truck and shouted, "Go!"

He floored the accelerator and the vehicle lunged forward like a bullet. She buckled up and collapsed against the seat. She'd made it.

Duncan was watching her truck, so she'd waited until he was doing his perimeter search on the far side of the yard and then she slipped out. Boomer had waited for her three blocks away. Even now Duncan was probably knocking on her door, wanting to know if she was all right. Too late now. She and Boomer were well out of sight. Mac would be angry. He didn't want her leaving the house for any reason. But she had to know Gloria was okay. She'd left Duncan a note on the coffee table. It wasn't like she'd left him completely in the dark.

"Hurry, Boomer," she pleaded. "I'm really worried about Gloria."

While she kept an eye out for the cops, Boomer made Brooklyn in record time. Gloria's sister lived in a cop neighborhood. Half the residents were on one force or the other, as her husband had been. When her husband died, Gloria had urged her to move to Manhattan with her but her sister had insisted on staying. Her neighbors were like family. She couldn't possibly leave.

"Just let me make sure someone is there," Elizabeth said when Boomer parked in front of the small, neat cottage. "I'll wave so you can go on if all is well."

"I can come in with you," he offered, his face scrunched with worry. "I don't like leaving you here."

"As long as Gloria is here, safe and sound, everything will be fine. I'll call Mac and let him know I'm here safely. He won't like it, but it's too late now. He'll send Agent Duncan on over." All of this could have been avoided if only Mac hadn't told Duncan to make sure she stayed put. She could have asked the agent to bring her here.

Boomer nodded reluctantly. I'll wait for your go-ahead."

"Okay." Elizabeth slung her purse on her shoulder, slid out of the truck. She walked to the front stoop and pressed the doorbell. Not sure if it worked, she followed with a couple of firm knocks. A moment later the door opened.

"Elizabeth?" Gloria frowned at her. "Are you all right?"

"Are you?" Elizabeth countered, quickly sensing the subtle differences in her friend's voice and posture. Something wasn't right.

Gloria started to say yes, but Elizabeth read the lie in her eyes a split second before she admitted defeat. "I can't do this anymore." She opened the door wider for Elizabeth to come in. "I have to tell you…"

Really worried now, Elizabeth waved at Boomer to send him on his way, and then she went inside. Gloria quickly locked the door behind her.

"Where's your sister?" Elizabeth asked. The silence in the house seemed to close in around them.

"I sent her and my niece away."

"What do you mean, you sent them away?" Fear inched its way into Elizabeth's heart. Things were definitely getting stranger by the second. Maybe she should have kept Boomer around a little longer. "Where are they?"

"I can't tell you, but they're safe from that madman." Gloria moved about the room, peeping between the slats of the blinds at window after window. "It's better if you don't know. I don't want him to find them."

Elizabeth moved to stand beside her friend as she peered out the front window. "What is it you have to tell me?" she asked softly, not wanting to push, but Gloria had said she had to tell her something. She suddenly wondered why the police officer who was supposed to be watching Gloria wasn't parked in front of the house. "Have the cops been by to see you?"

Gloria spun toward her. "No!" she practically shouted. "I haven't seen anyone."

This was too bizarre. "Gloria, tell me what's going on."

Her eyes glistened with emotion. "That bastard is after my niece. I had to save her. I don't care if he kills me."

Elizabeth had missed something here. This didn't make sense. "I don't understand."

"Ned, the son of a bitch, took advantage of my niece, too," Gloria cried.

At first Elizabeth wasn't sure what she meant, then she understood. "Oh, my God. Not Carrie."

Gloria nodded jerkily. "I couldn't believe it" She swiped at the tears falling freely now. "I wasn't really that surprised when he used us, but she's just a kid. Barely eighteen." Gloria shook with rage, her face turning beet-red. "She kept having all those problems after her father's death. Ned was certain he could help." Gloria clenched her jaw, a muscle jerking in her cheek. "He helped all right. Carrie didn't tell me how he took advantage of her until a couple of weeks ago."

Elizabeth put her arms around her friend and hugged her stiff shoulders. "I'm so sorry. You're right he was a bastard."

Gloria went completely rigid. "That's why I killed him."

For a couple of seconds her words didn't fully penetrate. When they did Elizabeth drew back. "Gloria, you can't mean that."

She pulled out of Elizabeth's arms and stared at her. "I did. I killed him." Her eyes were glassy now. "I'm glad he's dead." She turned away.

Elizabeth tried to gather her wits. What the hell did this mean? Could Gloria be serious? "Tell me what happened."

Gloria lifted one shoulder in a shrug. "I didn't actually mean to kill him. I went there to teach him a lesson. I screwed his damn brains out making him vulnerable, and then I pulled out my dead brother-in-law's service revolver." She laughed, the sound empty, so unlike her usual tinkling laughter. "He was scared shitless. I had him trussed up like a Christmas turkey in that chair, buck naked, and then I tortured him. Mentally, mostly."

She lapsed into silence for a time and Elizabeth struggled to be patient. Gloria needed her strength and her understanding. She had to allow her to get this out in her own time.

"He'd taken out that dagger you'd given him. Cleaning it or admiring it, who knows? Or maybe he intended to scare you with it when you showed up." A laugh tore out of her again. "I was there when you came over mad as hell that he'd stood you up. I was hiding in the master bathroom, praying you didn't find me. I couldn't hear everything you said...just parts. But what you said made me even more certain I had to make him pay. When you left and I tempted him into a game he couldn't resist. He loved every minute of it as I tied him up. He even liked it when I stuffed those panties in his mouth. I picked up the dagger and that's when he got worried. I taunted him with it, drew blood a couple of times just to hear him whimper." She paused for so long Elizabeth wasn't sure she intended to continue. "Then he laughed at me."

Her voice had gone arctic cold.

"I didn't mean to kill him…but I was so angry," she said tightly. "The next thing I knew the dagger was in his chest. I don't even remember doing it." She dragged in a shaky breath and exhaled loudly. "I don't remember anything after he started laughing except the look in his eyes when the blade sank into him. It made this…awful sound."

Elizabeth fought back the images her friend's words elicited. "Gloria, I know this is hard, but why didn't you call the police? You could have explained everything."

She whipped around, pinning Elizabeth to the spot with a piercing glare. "And then what? Spend the rest of my life in prison? For killing a piece of scum like him?"

"Okay, okay." Elizabeth held up her hands. "I understand. Hell, I would probably have done the same thing if it had been my niece."

"You would've?" Gloria's bravado wilted. "God, I can't believe I did it." She peered out the window again.

It was dark now and with only the dim slice of moon hanging in the sky there wasn't much she could see. Just a streetlight struggling valiantly to send its glow across the small expanse of grass in the yard.

"Those moments keep playing over and over in my head," Gloria said quietly. "I see myself doing it, but I still can't believe I did. It's like it really wasn't me, just someone using my body. I took the videos he'd made of Carrie and me. I couldn't find yours." She looked at Elizabeth in earnest. "I swear I tried to find it but I was so upset…"

"It's all right." Elizabeth thought about how Gloria had urged her not to tell the police anything, not to give them any extra information. She'd been trying to protect Elizabeth, as well as herself and her niece. But everything had gone wrong.

"Now he wants her dead," Gloria murmured. Her whole body seemed to quiver with a new, building emotion. "Well, I'll see him in hell first," she snarled. "Since it obviously wasn't Brian, I may not know who *he* is, but I'll be here waiting when he shows up."

Ignoring her resistance, Elizabeth pulled her friend into an embrace once more. "And I'll be here with you. If he comes, we'll take him on together."

Surrendering just a little, Gloria burrowed her face in Elizabeth's shoulder. "We have to!" she cried. "If we don't, he'll kill us all. I can't let him hurt Carrie. This is all my fault."

"No way," Elizabeth argued. "We're in this together and we'll be right here waiting for him. We'll get him." She prayed Duncan would get here or get word to Mac quickly. Elizabeth would fight to the death for her friend, but they needed backup.

Gloria drew away, her face cluttered with worry. "I'm sorry I let the police suspect you. I should have come forward. I should have at least told you." She blinked back a new surge of tears.

"It's okay." Elizabeth hugged her tightly. "It'll be over soon."

Elizabeth could almost feel him coming. Whoever he was. Things had been building toward this moment since Ned's death. The momentum had been unstoppable. She closed her eyes and prayed that God would keep an eye on them. Maybe Mac would swoop in and save the day.

Her courage shored up at the mere thought of him, Elizabeth looked at her friend. Why wait for Mac to get the word from Agent Duncan. She brushed away the tears glittering on her cheeks. "I think I'm going to stack the deck to our advantage."

Gloria frowned wearily. "What do you mean?"

"I'm going to call us a hero."

Mac was on the phone with forensics, pushing for a speedy analysis on the latest victim. He had a few last-minute details to handle and then he was going to Elizabeth. He didn't want her in anyone else's care tonight.

Of course her safety was of primary importance, but a major part of him wanted a repeat of last night. He wanted to make love to her over and over.

If he could just get these damned people to commit to a time.

The intercom buzzed, sending a fresh bolt of pain through his aching head.

"Agent MacBride, there's a call from Mexico for you on line four. And that other call is still holding on three. When I asked her if she wanted to continue holding, she said it was extremely important that she speak to you."

She? "Who is she?" The receptionist hadn't said a damned thing until now about the caller being a woman. His first thought was Elizabeth. But Duncan would have called if Elizabeth had needed anything.

"She wouldn't give her name."

Uneasiness sliding into his gut, he barked a thanks and stabbed the blinking button that represented line three. He could call forensics back. "MacBride." Nothing. The line was dead. The caller had hung up.

Mac swore and poked the final flashing light He'd been anticipating this call from Mexico all afternoon. He couldn't risk missing it. He needed confirmation Harrison's brother, his identical twin, was dead.

"MacBride."

"We've got your body, MacBride," Agent Hernandez who worked in Mexico as a liaison between the FBI and the CIA announced, "but I think you're going to be a little startled."

Why the hell not? Everything else about this case had been screwy. What was one more wacked out item on the list? "Let's hear it, Hernandez."

"Nigel Harrison may very well be dead, but he isn't buried here. The corpse in the coffin at his gravesite is female, and in damn good condition, too. Incredibly well preserved."

A woman. "Do you have any idea who she is and why she would have been buried in Harrison's stead?"

"Sure do and I have a nice thick file on Nigel Harrison. He was a rather naughty boy when he lived down here. When the Harrison brothers were growing up, they became close friends with another foster kid. A girl. According to the family who fostered the three, they were inseparable. Apparently their tendency toward dastardly deeds started way back then. If they got caught in something underhanded, not one would admit who actually did the deed. Loyalty was the mainstay. The three stayed in contact when they went off to college. Nigel and the woman became lawyers, and Ned became a doctor. All three apparently rose well above their beginnings."

Mac was becoming impatient. He knew some of that already. "So you don't know where the hell Nigel Harrison is or even if he's dead."

"That's right. He supposedly died in the jungle down here and his body was carried out by the cave dwellers his companion on the journey allegedly hired."

Mac swore viciously. "I have to find him," he muttered. "Why would he have faked his death?"

"I can't help you with where he's at," Hernandez admitted. "But I can speculate about why he faked his death. The corpse in the coffin belongs to a murder victim. Her throat had been slashed. She might have been well preserved, but the morticians down here aren't so good at covering up the cause of death. I imagine Nigel Harrison faked his own demise to conceal his handiwork. From the looks of the wound, he all but decapitated her."

Realization slammed into Mac. "You said you identified the woman buried in Harrison's grave?" Hell, she could be anybody, but he had a sneaking suspicion it was someone very close to the Harrison brothers.

"Oh, yes. Since her practice was in California and they fingerprint everyone who applies for a driver's license, her prints were on file."

Mac wished he could reach into the phone line and give the man a shake. "Do you have a name?"

"She was the girl who became the Harrison brothers' foster sister. Her name was Annabelle Ford."

"It's Annabelle," Elizabeth whispered as she peered through the door's peephole. "What do you want to do?" She'd have to try Mac again in a few minutes. She'd held on as long as she could. Maybe she should have given the receptionist her name, but she'd feared it would set off some sort of alarm since Agent Duncan had no doubt already called in. She'd had a heck of a time convincing Gloria to agree to her calling Mac. Gloria didn't want anyone to know their whereabouts. Paranoia had set in but good.

"Let me see." Gloria tiptoed to look for herself.

"I don't know, Gloria." Elizabeth tried to rationalize her hesitation. "I realize you trust Annabelle, but there's something wrong about her. The longer I think about it, the stronger the feeling."

Gloria wrung her hands as a fourth knock echoed, startling them both even though they'd known it was coming. "I...I guess we should let her in. She's a lawyer—she could help. She could have news."

Elizabeth still hesitated. "How well do you really know her?"

Gloria cradled her face in her hands for a moment, and then shrugged. "Not that well, but it seems like she's tried to help us from the beginning."

Maybe so. Pushing aside her nagging reservations, Elizabeth opened the door. "Hurry," she urged the older woman. "We don't want anyone to see us."

Annabelle hurried inside, the same look of desperation on her face that Elizabeth no doubt wore.

"There's been another murder," Annabelle said quickly. "I'm really getting worried. I'm not sure the authorities are going to be able to stop this."

Elizabeth hugged herself. "I'm wondering that myself." She studied Annabelle, tried to pinpoint the rub. What was it about her that nagged at Elizabeth?

Annabelle looked from one to the other, a worried expression on her face. "Are you two all right?"

Elizabeth and Gloria exchanged a hopeless look. "Well," Gloria began, "it's..."

"It's just that we're sick about this latest victim," Elizabeth said quickly. She suddenly didn't want Annabelle to know the truth. "One of us is probably next."

"That's why I'm here. I was worried about the two of you. I couldn't find you," she said to Elizabeth, "and I couldn't get either of you on the phone. This was the last place I knew to look. Thank God you're safe." She frowned. "But something isn't right here," she said slowly. "What's going on?"

"I killed him!" Gloria blurted, a new gush of tears punctuating the admission. "It was me. I...I..." Her words faltered, replaced by a high-pitched keening sound.

"It was an accident," Elizabeth hastened to add as she quickly enveloped her friend in her arms. "It's okay, Gloria. We'll explain everything to the police. There were extenuating circumstances."

"You don't get it," she wailed as she drew away from Elizabeth. "I screwed up! And now he's after my niece. She's the last one before the two of us."

Carrie Upton. Elizabeth shook her head in confusion. "But why wasn't she on Ned's patient log?"

"He agreed to keep her name off the record so her psychiatric care couldn't come back to haunt her. She's so young. I didn't want her to start out with that hanging over her head. You know the big corporations and even some of the universities look for things like that now."

Gloria's revelation explained why Mac couldn't find a name that came before W.

"And now she's in danger because of me!" Gloria trembled violently. "She may die because of my stupid mistake!"

Elizabeth reached for her friend to comfort her, but Annabelle got to her first.

"Don't worry, Gloria, you won't have to witness anything bad happening to your niece. I'll take care of everything." Annabelle smiled down at the shorter woman, the expression ominous somehow. "You can go first."

Before Elizabeth could react, Annabelle anchored Gloria against her body, holding her like a shield. Something glinted as her right hand went to Gloria's throat. "I don't mind deviating from the plan."

Knife.

"What're you doing?" Elizabeth shouted. Mac's description of arterial spray crashed into her brain. Her heart stumbled.

"Did you really think I'd let you get away with it?" Annabelle growled, her usually deep voice even deeper now. "I knew if I picked you off one at a time, I'd eventually get the right one. Of course I was well aware of the few who'd made an impact on my brother's emotions. The ones he toyed with the most...who resented him the most."

Elizabeth tried to make sense of the scene. Annabelle was threatening to kill them. Her voice had deepened considerably. She'd called Ned her brother.

Oh, God.

The twin.

"You're Nigel."

"Well, give the girl a star," she...*he* taunted, not even attempting to hide his masculinity now.

Elizabeth looked at his meticulous chignon and then at the perfect fit of his suit over undeniable mounds of breasts. The smooth, toned legs visible below the hem of the skirt. She'd known something wasn't right, but she never saw this coming.

"Take a good look, Elizabeth. It'll be your last." He laughed cruelly. "Just so you know, the hair is all mine. It took me four years to get it like this. Of course the color is different, just like my eye color. Aren't colored contacts marvelous?" He chuckled. "The breasts cost me a small fortune. Ned loved them." Nigel gave Elizabeth a knowing wink. "Since I'm still all man below the waist, he said I had the best of both worlds. A little facial surgery here and there and no one could tell I wasn't a woman or that we were brothers. It was our secret." He laughed, the vile sound sickened Elizabeth. "Even you didn't know."

"Why go to so much trouble to be someone else?" Elizabeth asked. She had to do something. But what? He could kill Gloria with nothing more than a flick of his wrist.

"It was either take over Annabelle's identity or admit that I'd killed her." He lifted one shoulder in a shrug of indifference. "Stupid bitch. She should have known I wouldn't marry her. But no, she refused to listen to reason. She wanted children. She was tired of all the games we played together all those years, just me, her and Ned. She'd heard her biological clock ticking. Tick tock," he sneered. "Too bad for her. I handled the dilemma masterfully, as I do all things. A little extra money to the mortician, one dirty cop, and *voila*. Alas, then I had to kill them both. I couldn't risk that one of them might grow a conscience one of these days and spill his guts."

Annabelle…Nigel…whoever the hell he was threw back his head and laughed at Elizabeth's horrified expression. She readied to take a dive at him. Gloria stood stock-still, frozen in fear, or perhaps defeat.

"Now," Nigel announced, snapping Elizabeth's full attention back to him and derailing her plan.

Dammit! She had to do something! "Why did you come here?" she demanded. "Why didn't you just stay dead?" Her fear gave way to anger. This monster had killed far too many already. He had to be stopped.

"To New York?" he mocked as if she was stupid. "Or *here?*" He looked down at Gloria briefly, and then leveled that satanic gaze back on Elizabeth. "I returned to New York to be with my brother, of course. We've never been apart for long. And everything was perfect until you bitches had to go and ruin it! You made him what he was. All of you. And that filthy Gentlemen's Association," he accused. "But they'll get theirs. Setting a little plan of revenge into motion was so easy."

Elizabeth knew what he meant. He'd set her up to lead Mac to the hidden room and, ultimately, to the Gentlemen's Association. "So he knew," she said, desperate to keep him distracted. "Ned knew you'd killed Annabelle."

Another round of hateful mirth. "Of course. He was glad to be rid of her, too. We always liked it better when it was just the two of us. As soon as I'm finished here it'll be just the two of us again."

Elizabeth fought to keep the fear from gaining control. Nigel was obviously insane. *Just keep him talking.* Her heart accelerated into overdrive. "How did you get into all those women's apartments? Did you use a gun?"

He smirked. "A gun wasn't necessary. All I had to do was tell them Ned had mentioned them in his will and that we needed to talk. It was ridiculously simple. They were all so stupid. Just like the two of you."

"Why…" Elizabeth fought to keep her voice steady, "why have you been pretending to help us?" Dear God, she was grasping at straws now. Her body was shaking…defeat dragged at her. How could this possibly end well?

"I needed you to help me lead the police to the association since they're part of the reason my brother's dead. They made him weak. You all have to pay. But just for the fun of it," he confessed with heinous delight, "I went in alphabetical order so I could save you for last. You were special to my brother, Elizabeth." His expression turned hard and cold. "Regrettably, the fun is over now. Ned wants me to finish this. It's time for him to see you die."

Out of time and options, Elizabeth lunged for him. Grabbed his right arm. Pulled with all her might. Gloria screamed, snapping from her paralysis and fighting to free herself.

With a demented roar Nigel shoved Gloria aside, the knife sliding through her flesh. Elizabeth saw the blood, tried to reach for her friend but Nigel blocked her path. She grabbed him by the hair, tried to knee him in the groin. She felt the cold bite of steel against her forearm. They struggled, falling the floor. The force of his weight coming down on top of her knocked the breath from her lungs.

He reared back, the knife poised high above her.

Elizabeth bucked, tried to throw him off. She clawed at him.

A crash echoed a fraction of a second before a gun blast filled the air.

Halfway to its destination the knife suddenly dropped from Nigel's limp hand.

He toppled backwards. Elizabeth shoved him off her legs and scrambled away. She rushed to her friend. Gloria clutched at her throat with both hands. Blood seeped between her fingers like crimson tears.

"I need an ambulance!"

Elizabeth swung her attention toward the sound. *Mac.* He'd shouted the order into his cell.

He'd saved them. Her hero had come.

As much as she wanted to dive into his strong arms, Gloria needed her more. As if reading her mind, Mac dropped to his knees beside Elizabeth and together they took care of her friend until help arrived.

Mac sat next to Elizabeth in the lobby of the surgical wing of New York General as she received the good news.

"Miss Weston will fully recover," the doctor explained. "The damage was primarily superficial. She'll need some cosmetic work in time but otherwise she'll be fine."

"Thank you." Elizabeth blinked at the tears but they slipped past her lashes anyway.

When the doctor walked away, she turned to Mac. Her bandaged forearm and the blood staining the front of her t-shirt vivid reminders of the horror she'd survived. "Thank God it's over," she murmured.

He slid an arm around her and pulled her close. "Amen."

They sat in exhausted silence for a while before she asked, "Mac, what will happen to Gloria?"

"That fancy lawyer you put on retainer will get her a deal."

Elizabeth looked up at him, hope daring to bloom in her chest. "Are you sure?"

He nodded. "Definitely. If he's half as good as his reputation, he'll sail through this on a temporary-insanity plea. Gloria admitted to you that she doesn't even remember thrusting that dagger into Harrison. She was out of her mind with worry for her niece. She went over the edge."

"Annabelle—Nigel," she amended, remembering those final moments, "kept talking like Ned was still with him."

Mac made a disgusted sound. "I think he went over the edge long ago—to the point of no return."

Elizabeth nestled against Mac's shoulder and prayed it would be that easy for Gloria to be cleared of what Ned, the bastard, had pushed her into. Her friend had made it past the first hurdle—she was going to recover. Now she just had to get through the legal clean up and closing of the case. Elizabeth would be there for her.

"What about the Gentlemen's Association?" She hoped they got theirs. Nigel had been right about their part in this tragedy.

"They're going down.

That was good news. She wanted them to pay for what they'd done. "What about us?" she asked without looking up. That question had haunted her all those long hours they'd waited to hear about Gloria. Worrying about her friend had kept her from focusing on the other.

But now, as relief sent the stress draining away, there it was.

Was this man going to break her heart?

Mac drew back and looked into her eyes. "I happen to know you have a problem with trust and, considering what you've been through, I can't blame you. I'd like to spend some time proving to you that you can count on me."

She smiled, her lips trembling with the effort of holding back a new wave of tears. "I already know I can count on you, Mac."

He pulled her close once more. "Then all we have to do is get to know each other better."

She smiled. "That sounds like a very good plan."

"We could leave for a little while now, you know," he whispered as he nuzzled the shell of her ear.

"Hmm…That would be nice but I'd like to be here when Gloria wakes up." Her breath caught when his tongue slid along her throat.

"Well," he blew on the wet path he'd made and her body quivered, "we'll just have to find ourselves a handy supply closet, because this isn't going to wait."

"Are you always this impatient, Agent MacBride?" she teased.

That blue gaze collided with hers. "I almost lost you today. Whatever's happening between us, it's special. Very special. I'm not about to waste any time, and I'm damn sure not going to risk losing you again."

His words touched her deeply. No one had ever made her feel this way. Mac was right. This was special.

His lips found hers once more, and just like before, the world fell away, leaving only her and the man she trusted with all her heart.

**If you enjoyed this story,
order your copy of SEE HIM DIE now!**

ABOUT THE AUTHOR

DEBRA WEBB, born in Alabama, wrote her first story at age nine and her first romance at thirteen. It wasn't until she spent three years working for the military behind the Iron Curtain—and a five-year stint with NASA—that she realized her true calling. A collision course between suspense and romance was set. Since then she has penned more than 100 novels including her internationally bestselling Faces of Evil series.

Visit Debra at www.debrawebb.com.
You can write to Debra at PO Box 10047,
Huntsville, AL, 35801.